Murder By Mustelidae

Written by: Serathin Sabertooth

Cover art by: Royz

Published by Smilodon Studio

Table of Contents:

Chapter One – The Job Offer

Winter… for some reason the cold seemed to settle in between the buildings far more than anywhere else, the normally bustling streets of the Windy City reduced to those brave few that needed to face the ice and snow to get to their destinations. Most settled in to their places of business or homes where walls kept Jack Frost from being an unwanted guest, and for one ferret those two spots were one in the same. The sound of a bottle being opened was the only thing that filled the air, followed by the liquid contents within making their way to a single solitary glass. The world outside was a cold, dark place and only the dim lights and quietly hissing radiator in the corner were the protections for this tiny city sanctuary.

Just as the stopper was put back into the bottle there was a knock at the door, rattling the frosted glass that had the name Alkali Bismuth on it as well as his occupation of Private Investigator. Though he wasn't one to shy away a potential client the ferret knew that anything could have come to his doorstep as he eased back in his chair as well as the hammer of his revolver next to his side. "Door's open," Alkali said as he kept his drink in one hand while he angled himself to the door.

When the sturdy wooden blockade to his threshold was eased back Alkali immediately relaxed his position slightly, though he continued to remain trained on the woman that walked through the door. The white-furred wolf-dog still had flecks of frost on her fur from the outside as she walked slowly in towards him. On first glance there didn't appear to be malicious intent in her eyes, one of which was brown while the other was blue, though as he continued to study her she seemed to take in her surroundings with innate curiosity. If she was a cat he would have a joke about that, Alkali mused to himself as he slowly put his sidearm back in his holster and brought himself back to sit completely upright.

"Was told that you were an ace detective," the wolf-dog said as she took a seat on the padded chair that was there for clients, slowly undoing the winter coat she wore to reveal a black dress underneath that was both simple and elegant. "Is this true, or are the letters on your door just for show?"

"Depends on who you ask," Alkali replied as he took a sip of the clear liquor before offering a glass to his impromptu guest, whom promptly declined. "Some say that I'm just someone who likes to get into trouble or the overly-inquisitive type, but since you're asking me and modesty doesn't pay the bills I would have to say that you heard correctly. What I'm wondering is what brought someone who looks ready to attend a fancy dinner party to trudge through the freezing cold all the way up to my office."

"It seems they're also right about you being overly-inquisitive," the wolf-dog said as she let a small grin cross her muzzle. "But that also something that I don't mind. My name is Trinity, though those who know me call me Momma T, and I want to hire you to investigate a robbery."

"A robbery?" Alkali repeated in slight surprise as Trinity gave a small nod in affirmation. "What did they take off with, your jewelry? Family heirloom?"

"Somewhere north of ten million dollars," Trinity replied nonchalantly. Despite attempting to retain his professionalism the ferret couldn't help but gawk at the sum that was so casually thrown out. How someone with that much could have it stolen from them was something that he didn't want to think about as he took another drink to stall while he attempted to figure out what to do or say next.

"As much as I would love to collect the fee for that I think you may want to go through the proper authorities," Alkali finally said after downing nearly half of his glass. "Since you're not hunched completely over I'm assuming you didn't just hide this money under your mattress, and with that assumption made I can make another one that the person who ripped you off was a highly-trained team. I may be good, but I'm only one ferret and I don't have the firepower to go up against whatever syndicate decided to rob you."

Alkali watched Trinity take the news by sighing softly and putting her hand to her forehead. "The problem with your assumption is that it's missing quite a bit of information," the wolf-dog said with a shake of her head. "The money that I'm talking about isn't mine, and it hasn't been stolen yet; a charity gala and auction are going to be robbed and when I looked into it there's going to be at least that amount in cash and items in one area. I heard some people talking about it at my day job, which is why I can't go to the police about it."

"I see…" Alkali said as he leaned back once more. "What is your day job Momma T, if I may inquire?"

"I'm a singer down at the gin joint a few blocks away called The Foxhole," the wolf-dog said as she motioned to the dress she wore. "I hope that doesn't break your heart that I didn't get dressed up just to see you."

"Given my usual clientele just having you sitting there is a breath of fresh air," Alkali stated. "I can also see why you can't exactly go to the police; they find out you overheard a few criminals at a local speakeasy about a crime that hasn't happened yet and it won't be the robbery they'll investigate."

"You understand my predicament," Trinity said. "Listen, let me fill you in on the details and you can decide on whether or not you want to take the job."

Alkali nodded and got the details of the crime that she had overheard, which wasn't too much. Two days ago just as Trinity was about to go onto the stage for her second set of the night she was coming back from the bar with a hot tea and honey, and just as she passed one of the private booths she heard the two talking about the charity gala. The wolf-dog pretended to powder nose and attempted to lean in to hear more, but all she managed to glean was still needing someone to pull off the last stage of the heist before they ended their conversation. Not wanting to be caught Trinity had finished her touch-up and moved as quickly as she could to the back stage before the two left and made her way up to the stage to not miss her cue.

The only other piece of information that Trinity could give the private investigator was that when she got on the stage she saw one of the two figures left, a smaller tiger man in a trench coat that slunk out of the back. It wasn't much but already Alkali was forming a list of potential people that it could be; he had a number of contacts in the seedy underbelly of this city, it was almost a necessity in his line of work. Once Trinity had finished she got up and gave him a small stack of bills that she said would be towards his fee as something to help him consider. She blew him a kiss and proceeded to saunter back out of his office, leaving him alone once more with only his thoughts and the last of his drink.

Once the door was closed Alkali looked at the wad of bills that had been given to him. It was certainly an unusual case; normally when he was called in to a robbery case it was an attempt to retrieve goods that the police either couldn't or wouldn't get back themselves. This was trying to prevent a crime from happening, and though he didn't like losing out on a paycheck the ferret still didn't know if he could pull something like this off. But it was to save a charity and it didn't hurt that he still felt the bills between his hands as he subconsciously counted them once more.

After a few minutes of sitting in silent contemplation Alkali finally came up with a solution that would be the best of both worlds. From what Trinity told him the gala wouldn't be up for another week so he could try to find some evidence that the police would listen too. It would be a dangerous game but he was always ready to play to win as he slowly stood up from his chair. He grabbed his coat off the back of his chair and started to walk out of the comfort that was his office into the chill night air.

The first instinct the detective had was to go to the speakeasy where the singer had first heard the conversation, but after thinking about it there was no guarantee that those two would be there again and that he could even locate them. Instead he decided to go after the lead on the tiger that Trinity saw, which combined with the fact that he was likely someone that facilitated in crime narrowed down the list of trees he would need to shake to find a lead. Criminals in this city were like cockroaches, for every one that he found there were dozens that hid in the shadows. All it took was to find the right roach, and as he walked down the street he could see that several were still out despite the cold.

It didn't take long and after talking to a few trusted contacts he narrowed it down to one likely suspect that brought him to a gambling den that took several hundred bucks and a favor to get into. They were often games protected by various syndicates and included alcohol as well. It made them prime targets for raids where the police could either show their teeth or shake them down for a bribe. Either way with the crackdown continuing on such places, especially since he could see the alcohol flowing, meant that they wouldn't those that were playing various card and dice games.

As the ferret eyed up the two large bear bouncers that had finally let him in past the steel security gate they gave him a small nod. There was an unspoken rule in the city underground; as long as you don't interrupt their business he was allowed to do his, especially since he mostly came into such places to remove troublemakers that would likely disrupt their operations. Of course if he was to ever call the police on this place not only would he lose the already difficult means of accessing such a place but he would be blacklisted from any other operation in the entire city and that would be the least of his concerns. That was why he frowned slightly when he saw a familiar face sitting at the small bar that was set up near the cashier station.

Though Alkali attempted to try and move around the other side of the impromptu casino that was in the old storage basement of the office building he saw the dragon he had tried to avoid turn his head to spot him. The ferret could do nothing but let the blue-scaled creature walk up to him with a small, knowing smirk. "Well well well," the dragon said as they leaned up against Alkali. "One of the city's top detectives showing up in a gambling den, I don't suppose I could get a scoop from you?"

"Why don't you go to Raisin Bran, they'll give you two Xander," Alkali replied as he went over towards the bar instead.

"Aw, don't be like that," Xander replied as they scooted up to the horse man cleaning glasses and ordered him a tequila. "Here, consider this my way for paying you back for that little debacle down at the Northside Dock, had I known that your investigation was still on-going I wouldn't have printed that."

"That little debacle cost me more than a few shots of tequila," Alkali replied as he grabbed the drink and downed it in one swallow. "But the real reason I don't need a reporter snooping around me right now is because I'm working a sensitive case right now. You want a story I'll write you a foreword; it involves a crime that hasn't been committed yet."

"The plot thickens," Xander stated as the grin remained on their muzzle. "Tell you what; I've already been here for nearly two hours trying to dig something up I can put into print, if I can help you with this little investigation of yours then you allow me to write a few chapters of this story for myself. It's either that or you start bugging a few people in here while they're trying to play and get the attention of management."

Alkali shuddered slightly at the mention of management, which for most people would mean someone's boss but in this case usually meant the gang that was running such an establishment. The ferret had no need to go up that high in order to find who he needed but Xander was right that it would be hard to find them in such a crowd. The fact that whomever was in charge allowed a reporter in meant that the dragon was deep enough in their pockets to find a ball of lint. After giving a small nod to the dragon and ordered another drink on his tab before walking further into the den.

A haze of smoke permeated the atmosphere to the point it burned Alkali's lungs worse than the freezing air outside as they passed the various tables. Even though it was none of his concern he couldn't help but see the stacks that people paid with and knew that these were serious gamblers. It was a thing of beauty, the ferret mused to himself, seeing gangsters and politicians playing together trying to win equally dirty money. But even being a gambling man he couldn't afford to look at those cards much less stack up chips against these hardened card players.

The one that the detective was looking for wasn't in the main pool of tables anyway; the tiger that he looked for worked on the other side, except instead of being a dealer he ran numbers for various sports games and other events that could be bet on. He was also the talent organizer for many of the criminal outfits that looked to work together for larger enterprises. Xander led Alkali to the back room where the smokiness and noise of the main area was left behind to a more private set of booths. As they came up to one near the back they passed by a crocodile that was getting up from the seat, his large snout scrunched up slightly as held his hat in his hands.

"I see you had another satisfied customer," Alkali said as he and Xander both sat where the other man had vacated, the tiger only looking up briefly while writing numbers down in a rather thick leather-bound book. "Do they all leave you that way?"

"Only the ones that lose," the tiger replied simply as he finished what he wrote before he put down the pen and looking up at the two with his gold-rimmed glasses. "I wouldn't believe those tears of his anyway, every week it's the same sob story and every week he's back here dropping another stack on another game. But I don't think that I'm getting a visit from the Ace Alkali just to ask about how I conduct my business."

"Only if you happen to be the one called Nizzbit," Alkali replied, the bookie giving a small nod. "Pleasure to meet you, could I get you a drink?" The tiger just took his fountain pen and tapped it against his glass that was half-full already of a clear liquid. "I see… then I suppose that we should get right down to business then."

"Time is money, Mr. Bismuth," Nizzbit stated as he put down the pen and took off his glasses to look at the two. "And I'm going to warn you right now that if it involves the affairs of anyone in this ledger you had better find someone else to squeeze, I won't ruin my reputation just so you can get the leverage on some cheating husband or degenerate gambler."

"It actually involves your other business," Alkali said, carefully choosing his words to avoid ruffling the fur of the already agitated feline. "Someone is setting up a job that is going to hit a charity gala for an eight-figure payday and something like that is going to require a lot of moving parts. All I need to know is who is pulling the strings."

There was a moment of surprise that crossed the tiger's face before he got serious once more, closing the book and taking a drink from his glass. "I knew a job like that wouldn't remain on down low for long," Nizzbit said with a sigh. "I was approached to run the logistics of that operation, yes, but I ended up turning it down a few days ago."

"Whoa, you turned down eight figures?" Xander exclaimed.

"Standard risk and reward assessment," Nizzbit responded. "Not to mention something about ripping off a charity didn't sit right with me. I did happen to set them up with a potential replacement for me that they were going to look into, a slightly less-disciplined but still effective man named Jimmy the Shark."

"I see…" Alkali said as he took a mental note. "He's a loan shark I take it?"

"No… he's an actual shark," Nizzbit stated, causing Alkali and Xander to look at one another before turning back to the feline. "Anyway I'll give you the details on this person in exchange for a favor, no doubt there will be someone that will try to hide from me in the future in order to avoid his debt that will need sniffing out. If that is acceptable then I would be more than happy to provide you with the information you seek."

The ferret frowned slightly at that; he knew the ramifications of owing someone in the underworld a favor, but that was one of the common currencies of this place and he knew that the tiger probably wouldn't accept anything else. With his case on the clock he found himself agreeing to the terms, which prompted the tiger to take a small piece of paper from a leather folder and wrote on it with his pen. Both Alkali and Xander waited in silence until Nizzbit had finished and then slid the note to the ferret, which only had an address and time on it. Fortunately the detective knew exactly what address that was and thanked the feline before taking the note and standing up.

Even though there was no name on the note it was more than enough information for Alkali to get started with. Nizzbit had set up a meeting with the one that was pulling off the heist and his potential replacement, and it happened to be in the same place that he had used the first time. While he wasn't fond of conducting business so close to where his client worked he really had no choice in the matter, and having someone that was already on board with the investigation could be a boon. As he got up however he noticed that he might be getting more help than he had realized when Xander started to follow him out of the back room and into the gambling den proper.

"Where do you think you're going?" Alkali asked as he went over to where he had checked his coat with the serpentine girl behind the steel cage where they held weapons as well as jackets.

"I hope your memory isn't that bad as a detective," the dragon replied as he slicked back his blue and white hair. "The people at the tables aren't the only one making deals here, or did you think that I was just going to be happy knowing that potentially one of the biggest heists is about to get busted and then wait around for the details? Plus I'm guessing that you still live in that little bedroom that is off of your office."

"Oh?" Alkali asked as a small grin crossed his face. "What's wrong with my office?"

"You shouldn't be mixing business with pleasure," Xander stated simply as they walked out into the frigid alley with a small nod from the bouncers while they passed by. "Plus my place is closer, unless you want to hoof it back to your place in the cold…"

The next day Alkali found himself looking out the window that led off of Xander's balcony, waiting for the water he had put on to boil while the dragon slept soundly in the other room. It had started to snow once more, but that was actually a good thing as it meant that the city was starting to warm up a little. Maybe it was a sign that his own case was starting to heat up, the detective thought to himself, or perhaps it was from the events that had preceded him standing there at that moment. Even though he could use a drink prohibition had made it near impossible for most to have a bottle or two of spirits on hand to satisfy such a need.

Fortunately that was going to change soon as the ferret watched the sun once more start to sink below the horizon of the city to enshroud the streets in darkness once more. The gin joint they were going to was seedier than a farmer's field in the spring, which meant that those who worked in such a place clocked in only when the moon was out. The only problem he would run into was that with his reputation everyone who saw him usually guessed that he was either working to ruin someone's day or expose them, and Xander wasn't going to be much more help since his status as a reporter was known. But from the small pool of people he trusted there was one that would blend in seamlessly with such a scene, one that he had already contacted in order to help him with this job.

Not wanting to compromise his inside man with them making a trip to the apartment of a known journalist Alkali had arranged for a meet-up at a greasy spoon that he had never frequented before. They were the best place to have a meeting since the one that sat next to someone at the diner counter could either be a complete stranger or their best friend. One thing he did know was that most of them had coffee so strong that it would bend the spoon that stirred it, which prompted him to make him and Xander a fresh pot before they went out. It was also a means for him to thank the dragon for their impromptu sleepover and as a means to wake both of them up for another night out on the town.

The smell of the fresh brew did wake Xander up as the dragon put on his bathrobe and the two of them shared a few cups while

Alkali told the reporter what was about to contact. While Xander was no stranger to the one they were about to meet the ferret needed to make sure that they had as little exposure between the three of them as possible. Alkali still needed to make sure that they were informed of the plan though so he had to make contact, the two of them finishing up their drinks before they heading out to the swirling snows outside. The diner was located only a few blocks away but every step they took was like icicles being drilled into their bone until it prompted them to take a cab the rest of the way.

A plume of steam rose up as the hot air from the diner escaped the door when Alkali opened it. The sounds of clattering silverware and the smell of cooking food filled the atmosphere as he walked inside, taking note of everyone that occupied the space. Most of them were people that were getting a bite to eat either heading from or to work under the fluorescent lights above. There was one notable exception though and that was the demonic imp that sat on the end of the counter looking through a menu, which was exactly what Alkali had told him to do at the dead drop they had set up.

Alkali watched the blue-scaled dragon walk around behind him and sit down at one of the nearby booths about a minute after he went in. The ferret wanted him to use his powers of observation in order to make sure their meeting wasn't disturbed, as well as be able to listen in on the conversation while making sure no one else did. Once he was in place the detective made his move as well, sitting down on the other side of the imp as they lit up a smoke. Even though the two remained nonchalant they shared a slight nod with one another as the wolfess that was serving the counter asked the ferret what he wanted.

"Pleasure to see you Draggor," Alkali said once the lupine walked off with an order of eggs and toast that hopefully wouldn't be greasier than the inside of an auto.

"You as well," Draggor replied as they took a drag before blowing out the smoke in a ring. "I have to say that when I saw a signal from you I was surprised, wasn't aware that you were working any big cases that involved my world."

"I caught one fresher than any of the ingredients you're going to find here," Alkali replied. "And the fact that you haven't heard any ripples yet from my presence is a good thing. I need you to play middleman for me, there's a meeting that I need to crash but as you know if I get within thirty feet of it I'm going to ring every alarm bell that they might have."

"You want me to ruin someone's day?" Draggor said with a slight smirk.

"I don't need you to burn the deal," Alkali quickly responded. "Quite the opposite in fact, we need it to go smoothly so that they don't know someone is looking onto them. We need to find out who the players are when it comes to this heist so I need you to try and get as much information as you can on the private meet, then report it back to me."

The demon chuckled and nodded his head slightly. "Boring, but doable," the demon said. "Not knowing the players is going to make this difficult though, I'm guessing you have a time and place?"

Alkali filled Draggor in on what the bookie had told him as well as peppering in the information that Trinity had given him, though he made sure that he didn't mention the wolf-dog. The last thing he wanted to do was get the singer involved any more than she already was, especially since she was working at the same speakeasy the meeting is taking place. Luckily Draggor caught on quick to what they were going to do and what his role in the operation was going to be. As soon as they had finished the details the imp stood up and paid his tab before leaving the counter and allowing the ferret to eat his meal alone.

While the ferret mildly enjoyed his eggs his mind wasn't focused on the flavor, being somewhat acutely aware of the slightly rubbery yolks moving around in his mouth just like the thoughts in his mind. He still felt somewhat uneasy that they were meddling in something so big, and part of him wondered if he was overreaching in his investigation. A million-dollar heist means big players, and those that they tail on this particular job might only be the pawns in the bigger game. But the detective had already put his own pieces into play and all he could do now was move them forward…

Chapter Two – Digging up the Dirt

With the same cold rearing its ugly head in the city and the sun no longer there in an attempt to banish it most found their way inside, one of which being the gin joint that Alkali headed towards. Crystals of ice formed on the fur of his chin as he held the collar of his coat up in order to try and shield his muzzle from the bitter winds. It was one of those times that having fur was a blessing, especially as he watched those with scales bundled up in so many layers they looked like a giant marshmallow as they passed by him. He imagined someone bumping into them and causing them to roll down the street with no ability to stop themselves, which caused a small smile to briefly cross his face before it hardened once more.

Focus on the case, Alkali thought to himself as he got to the door lit up by fluorescent neon. Despite its façade of being a dry jazz club he could already see the subtle advertisements that marked it as a common speakeasy. A simple scratch on the wall here, a chalk drawing of a broken booze bottle or a series of x's there; as a drinker himself he had long since been in the know on what to look for to differentiate the booze dens from their upstanding and law-abiding counterparts. The ferret wondered how such a code hadn't been broken by the police yet, but knowing a few that liked to have a nightcap of their own he guessed that they either didn't care or relied on them just as much as the citizens of this city.

As he took out his pocket watch from his breast pocket and flipped the steel cover open he saw that it was almost eleven. The meeting wasn't for another half-hour, but he wanted to make sure he could blend himself into the scenery as much as possible and avoid being caught by eyes that would recognize him. Draggor likely was already inside to establish himself, a criminal being seen in such a place was hardly a blip on anyone's radar, and Xander would be resigned to the back alley to try and tail anyone that escaped the demon's net. That just left him to cover the front, which he would do from the inside so he wouldn't end up frozen like his draconic counterpart as he walked inside.

Unlike the gambling den that he had previously visited there was no one there to check his weapons; instead he got the usual stare from the rather burly reindeer man who had to duck down to keep his antlers from hitting the ceiling as he sized the ferret up. A place like this valued privacy over all else and Alkali imagined if there was a police raid this guy could just stick his head in the door and keep them jammed for hours. Fortunately this was one time that being recognized was a good thing as the bouncer knew him and merely gave him a warning not to cause trouble before allowing him access. That was one thing that Alkali was definitely planning not to do, the detective thought to himself as he walked through the inner door.

The Fox Hole was one of those bars that you wouldn't plan on going to, like most of the people inside they likely wandered in by accident and thought that it was good enough. Or perhaps they merely stuck to the floor like the ferret's shoes as he wandered his way over towards the bar. He didn't see any spirits on the shelves and knew that no speakeasy in their right mind would be that brazen, except for ones owned by the various gangs that populated the area, but as he went up and sat down on one the stools the unmistakable odor wafted up from the glasses of those that sat next to him. As he waited for the bartender to notice him the ferret took a glance around the rest of the place to see if he could see either Draggor or Jimmy the Shark.

What he saw instead was a familiar face coming up to the stage, a spotlight darkening the rest of the room around the figure as several hoots and whistles came up from the crowd. It was the unmistakable look of Trinity as she went up to the microphone and began to sing while the band behind her accompanied with a smooth jazz beat. The dress she wore was not the same one that he had seen her wearing in the office, this get-up a sequined-riddled purple number with a flowery light purple feather boa around her neck. She had the presence of some starlet and Alkali wondered why someone who should be surrounded by velvet curtains and champagne was instead in an atmosphere of cigar smoke and bathtub bourbon.

"Hey, Alkali," a voice suddenly tore the ferret's attention away from the stage and the dog-wolf that occupied it, turning his head to see a fox man staring right at him. It was Zen, the proprietor of this small establishment as well as bartender and skull cracker if the need arose. While he wasn't sure he would call the vulpine a friend they knew each other well enough that Alkali wouldn't cause trouble in exchange for allowing the ferret to operate in his bar. "You keep gawking like that I'm going to start to think you're not here to drink."

"Would hate for you to get the wrong impression," the ferret replied. "Give me the usual with a lot of ice." He got a rueful look from Zen, who knew that the detective only ordered his drink like that if he was on the job to avoid becoming too sloshed. "By the way, have you noticed any usual characters that have come in, perhaps someone of an… aquatic nature?"

Alkali didn't want to get too specific in case someone happened to bend an ear in his direction, but it also caused the fox to just give him an incredulous look. "I'm a barman, not a census taker," Zen said back as he mixed the drink. "Plus thanks to the raid that happened to the place a few blocks from here I'm up to my armpits in barfly refugees. You're going to have to do your own looking around."

Though that wasn't the answer that the detective was hoping for it was something that he had expected. He didn't want to press the fox much further and accidently tip his hand, but as he looked around the dark, smoky interior of the bar it was hard to distinguish the faces apart even with a particular species in mind. The one thing that did cause him some sense of relief was the familiar visage of the imp near the back at one of the tables. Draggor had struck up a game of cards with a few others and from the way the imp was positioned it was clear they had chosen the seat to keep an eye on the private booths that were just on the other side of the room.

The ferret remained in his seat where he could see the front of the house while sipping on his drink, the sting of alcohol on his tongue causing him to blink a few times. Unlike the personal stash he kept at home, which had been made before prohibition had started, this was clearly the product of some bootlegger that resided in the outskirts of the city limits. He could only guess how many impromptu distilleries were set up in the national park that bordered one side of this city, though occasionally he would hear about some fire or explosion that was caused by the improper handling of spirits. When one went down two more would spring up in their place, which was probably why the police appeared to be so flustered in dealing with this alcoholic hydra on their hands.

Fortunately Zen appeared to have at least found one that knew what they were doing enough that he wasn't worried about going blind, but it was still a potent cocktail and he had half an hour to spare before their contact arrived. Trinity continued to sing for a while before leaving for a break, which left the jazz band to continue on their own. When Alkali looked down at his pocket watch once more he saw that it was nearly time for the meeting to happen, which caused him to glance back up and look over at the private booths. There were four that Zen made available for private engagements and two of them were open, and Alkali wondered if the one that was behind this heist had been there the entire time. He still had no idea who they were looking for though and part of him wished he had pressed the tiger on more information before they had started this potential wild goose chase.

Once more he looked down at the face of his watch, watching the big hand slowly move past the six and move on to the next dash. It felt as if he was attempting to summon this shark by staring at his watch but no one matching that description came through the doors. Had Nizzbit possibly set them up, or had the robbers gotten wise that a detective was on their tail? All potential scenarios ran through his mind and as he looked over at where Draggor was sitting he could tell they were having similar thoughts. The last thing that he wanted to go back to the client with was nothing but this was their only lead and it appeared to be a dead-end.

Just as Alkali was about to get up from his position and check outside the outside door opened once more. The cold air that blew in made currents in the smoke that hung around the atmosphere, and the figure that stepped through slowly revealed himself to be a shark as he took off his hat. The ferret could feel his heart start to pound harder as he watched the mark slowly walk in and make their way back towards the private rooms. Other than being late this guy looked to be everything that someone might need to pull off a robbery, the detective taking note of the scarred eye on his grim demeanor. Glancing over at the imp he saw that they had also taken note of the aquatic creature and had started to wrap up his card game.

As much as the detective wanted to be in on this he knew he couldn't bust up the criminal interview now. If either the shark or the one he was meeting remained in the bar then Draggor would attempt to chat them up and try to find more information, and if either left through the front or rear exit then it was up to himself or Xander to follow them to try and find their base of operations or another contact. He wasn't a fan of being hands off like this but the last thing Alkali needed to be was on the blacklist of some criminal enterprise that was pulling off a heist as big as this. It still didn't calm his nerves though and part of him wished that the fox had not filled his cup all the way to the brim with ice as he took out a cube and chewed on it anxiously.

Less than fifteen minutes passed before the curtain the shark had pulled closed after entering the private booth slid back again, the same creature leaving in a huff. It appeared the meeting had not gone so well, at least that's what his senses were telling him. The criminal immediately went over to the bar and pounded his fist on the already cracked wood, demanding a drink loudly. Though Zen got a sour look on his face he quickly went over and took his order while Alkali slowly got up from his seat. Draggor had already started to move in the direction of the bar to intercept Jimmy, which left him free to help with the one that had conducted the questioning.

Since he probably hadn't been invited on board it was unlikely that the shark would know anything of use to them except the identity of the one that he talked to, Alkali reasoned, which meant that their only hope was to follow the one already involved. He still didn't want to be seen by the perpetrator and took a roundabout way of getting to the private rooms, but as he did so there was something that had started to agitate his detective senses. The interview had been over for almost five minutes now but there was no movement inside the booth that the shark had stomped out of. As he continued to approach he saw that the curtain hadn't been completely closed and if he got just the right angle he found himself able to see inside…

…to a completely empty booth.

Alkali's heart dropped to his chest and he rushed over towards it, flinging the curtain back completely to find the only thing that occupied the space were the cracked vinyl of the booth and a single candle that had been snuffed out. How? Even when Jimmy had made a spectacle of himself by stomping over to the bar he had continued to keep an eye on the space. Surely even in his distracted state he would have seen someone open the curtain and leave, unless…

It took less than a minute of searching before Alklai pulled the cushion of the booth next to the wall up and saw a dark, foreboding space that led downward. It was a tunnel; one that the patrons could use in the case of a police raid that Zen no doubt shared with his more privileged clients. He made a mental note to talk to the wily fox bartender later as the ferret jumped down into the hole he had just uncovered. It wasn't very deep and the temperature shifted dramatically as he quickly felt solid stone beneath his feet.

In front of Alkali was a tunnel that had been clearly hand-dug with a string of lights that illuminated the cramped space. With as tall as he was the ferret had to crouch and suck in his stomach on multiple occasions in order to get through it. Luckily for him it was only about ten meters and when he emerged he found himself in the root cellar of a nearby building that he knew to be abandoned. From there it didn't take long to retrace the criminal's steps and eventually he saw a ray of street light shine in from a pair of closed doors. Just as he started to go up the stairs however he heard a loud pop, his ears perking up as the muffled gunshot echoed slightly in the stone basement he had found himself in.

Almost immediately his first thought was that Xander had been made and it caused the adrenaline in his system to spike. The rotted wooden stairs protested loudly under his heavy footsteps as he raced his way up and barreled through the metal doors. There hadn't been anything holding them shut and they flew open with a bang, revealing a vacant lot that was littered with trash and metal scrap. There had been no follow-up shots and Alkali knew the dragon didn't have a gun on him, the ferret pulling out his own before heading in the direction he believed the shot came from.

When he hopped over the short fence that divided the alley from the vacant lot Alkali realized that he was where the gin joint exited in the back. A cloudy breath of relief escaped the ferret's muzzle when he saw that Xander was still up on his feet, though it quickly turned to confusion when he also saw Trinity there and the two were running towards him. "What on earth happened!?" Alkali shouted at them as he quickly looked around for the potential assailant.

"Don't blame me!" the dragon quickly exclaimed, the two still running as they motioned a thumb to the wolf-dog next to them. "I saw someone head out of the lot you just came from and was about to follow when this one got involved!"

"I thought you had let him get away!" Trinity shouted back. "Just like you two will now if we don't chase him!"

Damn… the last thing that Alkali wanted to hear was that Trinity had gotten involved in the investigation, and as they passed by him and he saw a snub-nosed .38 in her hand he quickly pieced together the events of what happened. She had probably saw him at the bar while she was singing and thought that they were letting the culprit get away, especially if she had seen him somehow use the secret passage out. Anything further than that was pure speculation, but it was likely that she confronted their criminal and had attempted to either detain them herself or tried to get information at the end of the revolver she was packing.

Unfortunately not only did the man appear to have gotten away but she had tipped their hand that someone was on to them, which meant if they let him go and he informed the others this crew would go to ground and they wouldn't know anything about their plan.

As the three of them got to the end of the alley it was just in time to see the other man, who appeared to be some sort of wolf on Alkali's quick observation, get into a car and start it up. They had no chance in catching it as they continued to run forward and could only watch as it began to drive down the alley towards the main street. This definitely was a rotten turn, the ferret thought to himself, but as he looked around he saw something that could change their luck for the better. The car that the one they were perusing had used to escape wasn't the only one that was in the lobby and the engine was already running on the truck as they came up to it.

"Hey, hey you!" Alkali shouted as they bolted towards the vehicle, watching the panda's head turn up towards them while he started to step inside. "We need your truck!"

"What, does this look like some sort of taxi service to you?" the panda replied as he brushed his mustache with his finger, closing the door behind him just as the three came up. "Get lost, I don't need you making all that racket around my car."

Alkali grimaced slightly as he realized that the seconds they using to deal with this driver were allowing the culprit to get further away, but before he could say anything Trinity reached into her dress and pulled out a slightly wrinkled bill. "How about this?" the wolf-dog said as the other two watched her pass the hundred-dollar note to him in slight shock. "Does that make you a taxi now?"

"Well paint me yellow and put a light on my hood," the panda said with a grin as he looked at the bill before motioning for her to get in. "The Pandez Express is at your service." Just as Alkali and Xander were about to climb into the cab as well the driver quickly wagged a finger at them to get them to stop. "Paying fares only up front, you two can get in back though."

Once again Alkali found himself not able to argue anything as he and his draconic companion quickly went around to the back and hopped between the back tailgate and tarp of the truck to get inside. No sooner had they done that then the vehicle started to drive, accelerating with surprising speed in order to get out of the alley and back into the streets proper. The two had to hold onto the barrels that were stacked in the sides as a sharp turn was made and the chase was on, the detective hoping that Trinity had gotten a good enough look at the escape car to follow. At the moment there was nothing that he could do except sit and wait, though as the vehicle reached cruising speed they suddenly saw a small viewing door between the back and cab of the truck open.

"You two alright back there?" Trinity asked.

"Aside from the shake-up when we started I think so," Xander commented as they got into a more comfortable position between the wooden barrels. "What do you have in this truck, a rocket engine?"

"Just a little something to help me with my deliveries," the panda replied, his head still facing traffic as he navigated his way through the mostly-empty streets of the city at night. "Had a few friends modify everything on this truck top to bottom; it may have the body of a truck but it has the soul of a plane. Anyway you two just get yourselves into a good seat and make sure you don't touch the merchandise."

Even without the sound of liquid sloshing against the insides of the barrels it was clear to the detective what this panda was running, especially at the mention of a souped-up car. This panda, who formally introduced himself as Pandez, was definitely a bootlegger. Ever since the start of prohibition there had been a race between bootleggers and cops; the former attempted to keep their shipments safe and outrun the latter that were trying to catch them. The ferret was certain that the bootleggers were probably winning this one, especially with the way he felt the trunk perform while they continued to pursue their target.

It was hard for Alkali and Xander to know exactly where they were heading, but as the minutes ticked by the ferret found himself growing more and more restless until finally he crawled his way over towards the window and poked his muzzle out of it. "So as long as our new friend here doesn't mind," Alkali said, glancing over at Pandez who continued to look out the window before going back towards Trinity. "You want to spill the beans on what you were doing in that vacant lot with a .38?"

"When you came into the bar I suspected that there was another meeting that might be taking place," Trinity explained with a small sigh. "I also knew that Zen had mentioned something about making sure that the secret tunnels that ran under the bar were free and ready to be used, so it didn't take much for me to put two and two together. When I took my break I decided to go back out into the vacant lot where the tunnels came out of and when I saw the wolf in a nice suit leave through the cellar doors there was no time to warn you of them."

"That wasn't very smart," Xander chimed in. "Even armed like that you put yourself in a dangerous position, he could have taken the gun from you if he didn't think that you would use it."

"Oh, I made sure he knew I was willing to use it when I put a bullet in his foot," Trinity replied. "But before I could get him to talk we both heard someone else coming through the tunnels, and in that moment of distraction he somehow managed to hop the fence and escape down the alley. It's just as well though, we're on his trail now and I doubt he's thinking very clearly at the moment."

Alkali balked slightly that the sweet, demure wolf-dog that had been in his office was not the helpless singer that he had first chalked her up to be. In fact there was something about it that caused his investigative nose to itch; if she was so capable of handling this thug than why hadn't she done so in the first place? If she was able to plug a guy in the foot from a few meters away then she certainly had some skill with the weapon and to so brazenly discharge it in the middle of the city was either foolish or a well-calculated move. He knew for a fact that even if they hadn't gotten a ride from the panda bootlegger they could have easily escaped the scene before any cop car would have decided to show up there to investigate.

With nothing else to ask Alkali closed the door and went over towards the opposite end of the cab where Xander sat. "A fierce one to be sure," the dragon commented as the ferret settled down as comfortably as he could. "Also there is something odd about this entire situation."

"Yeah, this is a side of her I didn't see when I took the job," Alkali admitted, though he saw the dragon shake their head at that.

"No, not her personality," Xander replied. "I've interviewed harder women then that, especially those that make their careers at those speakeasies. Don't you find it a little strange that she just happened to have a hundred dollars on her person for being a singer at some lowly jazz club?"

Alkali was about to respond when he realized that the dragon was right and reminded him of the payment he had gotten when they first met. At first the ferret had assumed that someone might have helped her bankroll his fee, but when he thought about the thick stack of green-backs that currently sat in his wall safe he began to wonder about its origin. He hadn't even counted it because he wanted to help more for the charity sake then his own payment, but if all those bills had been hundreds then he had gotten paid at least three times his usual fee. There was definitely something about this that didn't smell right, but all the detective had at this point was smoke and mirrors and he couldn't conjecture anything else until he finally found his feet on solid evidentiary ground.

That footing came when the truck came to a stop, the metal door sliding open again with Pandez announcing that they had followed the truck all the way to the entrance of the dockyards where most of the shipping for the city went through. As soon as Alkali looked out from the tarp he could see the car they had been chasing was parked roughly to the side near one of the buildings. "I hope you don't mind if you three take a real cab home," Pandez said as the three of them piled out of the truck, the panda adjusting his top hat to them as they walked to the front. "This puts me behind and if I don't bring her back before the sun rises the others get a little nervous."

Pandez patted the side of the truck door and Alkali told him it was alright and he could go, which immediately prompted the rum runner to reverse back until he could turn and drive down the road. Though the ferret wasn't fond of being at the dockyards in the middle of the night without any way to quickly escape the presence of the bootlegger's truck would only serve to alert anyone that was watching, if it hadn't already done so. Fortunately a fog thicker than the blankets at home the ferret wanted to be under at that moment had started to roll in from the bay that had caused their approach to be obscured, though it also meant that they couldn't see exactly where the wolf had gone after he pulled into the dockyard and got out of his car. With only one to get in and out of the place Alkali felt confident they could catch their bad guy unaware in what he hoped was their lair.

"Do you think that we should split up?" Xander asked as he tried to peer through the fox that covered the entirety of the yard while they walked over towards the other parked vehicle.

"Not in this weather," Alkali replied. "If one of us does find the wolf then it would probably take longer to find us than it would if we stuck together. Luckily I think I know of way that we can easily track him down, the perp was nice enough to leave us a trail of breadcrumbs."

The other two looked at the ferret in question as he stared down at the ground, then followed his gaze to the concrete. On the cracked white surface of the decaying stone they saw a bright patch of red in the shape of a partial footprint on the ground. There were several more that followed it and from the way they were positioned Alkali could tell that the one they were following was limping from the pain. It was yet another indicator they had the right person and they could capture them without trouble… as long as they were the only person here and not with whatever gang holed up here like rats.

While they continued to follow the path of the blood Alkali kept a look-out for anything that might indicate that there were more people there than just the injured wolf, but to his relief there were no other cars than the one they had passed initially. Even with nothing standing out to him he pulled out his gun and kept it at his side as the three of them made their way from building to building. As they got to one corner and pressed against the crumbling brick he noticed out of the corner of his eye that Trinity had her own weapon ready, but instead of telling her to put it away he decided to let the hybrid keep her steel just in case. That just left Xander who remained between the two since they didn't have anything as Alkali peered around the corner and saw that the trail ended at the door where a single light shined through a grimy window.

Alkali instructed the two to remain behind and allow him to check out the warehouse for himself, and though Trinity clearly wasn't fond of that idea she nodded and held back along with Xander. The detective darted around the corner and quickly ran between the two buildings, and for the first time he realized how cold it still was as his coat flapped around him. He suddenly became acutely aware of how numb his fingers had gotten pressed against the chilled metal of his weapon, but he was in no position to do anything but find the next spot to hide in as he approached the door. When he got to the door he looked through the nearby window to see if he could see anything about who was inside, but other than shadows that flitted about to indicate someone was in there the years of grime on the glass made it impossible to see anything else.

Instead of risking being spotted by trying to find another entrance Alkali decided to go the direct route, holding his pistol out with one hand while the other slowly moved to grab onto the door handle. There would be no quiet way to do this, especially if the door was being watched, so the ferret moved with purpose and swung the door open before shifting his body to see inside while also aiming his gun. On his observation the door had led to a small shipping office and the shadows he had seen was the flickering of the lit candle behind some shelves. There was no one else inside as Alkali closed the door behind him, but as he walked inside and let the door close behind him he could see that there were a number of bloody footprints that were spread about.

But where did he go, Alkali mused as he walked forward and looked at the chair that had been dragged out to the middle of the room. There were a number of medical supplies that were on the ground including a bowl of red-tinted water and a large roll of bandages that someone had recently used. There was also a bloody shoe with a hole in it that was next to the ground as well. But as Alkali took in his surroundings more he realized that wasn't the most interesting thing in the room.

Before the detective could do anything though he heard a click, the telltale sound of a hammer being cocked back echoed in his ears as Alkali slowly lifted his hands. Even though he remained still he saw on the reflection of the glass on the inside of the office that the wolf aimed at him from a door that was partially obscured by the rows of shelves when he had come in. "Well, you must be Alkali," the wolf said as the door opened more fully and the lupine limped out. "I was told that I might possibly run into you."

"By who?" Alkali asked, his investigative instinct kicking in even with having a gun drawn on him. "Who do you work for?"

To the ferret's surprise the wolf lowered his weapon and moved over to his coat, fishing something out of his pocket that he threw on the ground in front of Alkali. "My name is Agent Poker Wolf," the wolf said as Alkali looked down to see the shiny metal gleam of a badge where the wallet had opened. "And you're interfering with a bureau investigation, Detective Bismuth."

Chapter Three – The Other Shoe

Alkali continued to look at the badge that had been presented to him in shock as Poker limped back over to the chair and sat down, the ferret watching the badge as though it would disappear at any second. He reread the letters FBI engraved on it multiple times and still couldn't believe they were stamped on there, especially belonging to someone that he thought was about to pull a major heist. It looked too good to be a fake though and he knew that there weren't many that would be crazy enough to impersonate a federal agency. But all this license did was act as a can opener, releasing dozens more questions in the air that he wasn't sure he would get answered… or even if he wanted to get involved with.

"You keep staring at that thing so intensely you're going to burn a hole through my wallet," Poker said, which prompted Alkali to walk back over and give it to him. "I'm sure that you don't have to go any further than that in order to establish my identity."

"No, I think that'll about do it," Alkali replied as he shook his head slightly. His eyes continued to glance over at the folders that were strewn about on the desk, all of them also marked with the logo of the bureau on them. "I know that you're probably going to say that it's sensitive information, but what is an agent doing pretending to try and recruit people to rob from a charity gala?"

For a moment Alkali thought that he might be absolutely correct that he wasn't going to be told anything, but to his surprise the wolf once more got up with a groan and motioned for him to follow as he hobbled over to the table. "It's not the charity gala that we're targeting," Poker stated as he handed Alkali a file, which when he opened it showed a brochure for the gala as well as a few other pieces of paper. "As far as we're concerned that's a legitimate event. What we are targeting is those responsible for pulling it off… I don't suppose you've heard of the Kage Syndicate?"

"That's who you're going after?!" Alkali nearly shouted, though Poker angrily motioned for him to keep his voice down. "Are you crazy, that group and its members organize half the illegal activities that go on in this city."

"Exactly my point," Poker replied as he showed Alkali a picture of an anthro cockroach dressed in a three-piece business suit. "If we could find a way to find a lead between the speakeasies, the gambling dens, and the gang itself we could form a rico warrant and dismantle most of the crime in this city, or at least the major players. The fact that you're snooping around my business means that I must be starting to make waves, if I'm lucky that means that I'll be getting a direct line with the gang itself soon."

"The only thing that you're going to be getting a line on is an express route into the harbor over there," Alkali stated. "Also I got nothing to do with them, someone overheard your plans and hired me in order to figure out what you're doing since you've posted that you're attempting to steal from a charity."

To the detective's surprise the wolf scoffed at that, then shook his head. "If you're talking about that singer that decided to give me a lead pedicure, you might not be as good a detective as I thought," Poker stated, and though it looked like he wanted to say more there was a noise that caused his ears to perk up. "Let me guess, she came with you, didn't she? You know what, it doesn't matter, I need to bury this badge and all the evidence here so it doesn't blow my cover."

"Hey, wait a second," Alkali said as he watched the wolf wince while moving to a sewer grate under the table and popped it open before throwing the badge inside, then started to do the same with the files on the desk. "Yeah, Trinity came with me along with Xander, but like I said all she did was overhear what you were doing. I think I would have suspected if she was a member of the Kage Syndicate."

Even though he said that to the panicking lupine though Alkali knew that there were inconsistencies adding up in the wolf-dog's story even before he found out about the undercover operation.

Had she hired him just so the Syndicate could figure out if someone was actually trying to rob from them? He did have a policy of not involving himself in gang business, something that most of the criminal underworld knew about according to Draggor. But a dame in a dress concerned about the safety of a prestigious charity event? If this was the case they knew how to push his buttons.

It was clear from his standing in the middle of this warehouse that if this was a lark he had fallen for it completely. "Hey, you still with me there Alkali?" Poker's voice rang out, Alkali not even realizing that the wolf had started talking to him again until that moment. "I was just telling you that there was a reason I was operating out of that gin joint in particular, our intelligence has told us that it's a place where a number of Syndicate members hang out. I wouldn't be surprised if Momma T is their canary, making sure that people like me don't hang around to try and get information from anyone. But we can talk about this later, right now I need you to go out there and tell the other two that you looked high and low but that I must have been picked up by a car and already left."

"What, why?" Alkali asked, surprised by the request being made of him.

"I'm not going to let two months of work go down the drain because my identity got leaked early," Poker replied resolutely. "I already have several leads from my dealings that can help with how the Kage Syndicate operates around this city, but if they know an agent is on to them then they'll immediately change the logistics around to protect themselves. So you need to go out there and lie to them that I was ever here, and then later on the two of us can meet at my real safehouse so I can debrief you. You're an official part of this investigation now and to be honest I could use someone of your resources to help me since I can't get much in the way of bureau assets."

Alkali frowned at that as he watched Poker take a can of red paint and dump it over the bloodstains on the floor as the last means of disguising his trail. He liked working for the cops even less than working for the gangs, and the FBI was no exception to that. Unfortunately it appeared that he had stuck his nose into something bigger than even he had expected, which meant if he didn't at least play along then they could make his life miserable. By this point it was possible that Xander and Trinity had also started to get suspicious of how long he had been in here scoping out the place.

"Alright, fine," the ferret grumbled. "But let's meet in my office instead, it'll be less out of place for someone to visit me there than for me to go off into some other section of town, especially if I'm being watched. I better be getting one heck of a commission for helping you out on this."

The wolf just smirked at him and gave him a small nod, then pointed at the door where he had come in the first place. Alkali left Poker to finish off the last of his cleaning detail and went outside to try and fabricate a story of what he had seen. Somehow he had to explain the light that was on in there as well as the wet paint that was splattered all around, something he didn't really want to do. He still couldn't believe that it was possible the woman who had come into his office asking for help last night was actually working for one of the largest criminal organizations in the city, but he couldn't be sure of anything until he got more information.

The bitter wind that slapped the ferret in the face as he left the warehouse served to help clear his senses and bring him back to the task at hand. He could figure out everything later, Alkali thought to himself as he looked around to see if the others had moved from their spot, for now he had to deal with the situation at hand. At the moment he would have to go along with the FBI agent and make sure that he wouldn't go to jail for impeding an investigation, especially since his involvement had already gotten Poker shot in the foot. Once he had gotten more information from him in their next meeting he could tell the wolf whether or not he wanted to be a part of it, and in the meantime he could possibly get more information on Trinity and the gin joint that he was operating out of.

The idea of being in the middle of something between the criminal underworld and the law still left a bad taste in his mouth, but extracting himself from a job like this without ruffling feathers was going to be harder than simply returning the money. It was the curse that came from being good at his job; with him being a player in the mix there were those on both sides that wanted to make use of his skills to make sure they won. There was also the possibility that he was being lied to by the wolf as well, even if he was a member of the FBI it didn't mean he couldn't be dirty or even on some sort of vendetta. Alkali could hear the thin ice practically cracking underneath his feet as he walked across the parking lot to where he had left the other two.

Much to his relief both Xander and Trinity were still there, the dragon poking his head out from behind the corner while the wolf-dog was further inside to use the building as a wind breaker. "It's about time you got here," Trinity said with a huff as she clutched her jacket to her body. "Any longer and you'd be talking to two popsicles. Was the guy in there or not?"

"If he was there he isn't anymore," Alkali lied, using the chill in the air to help steel his face as Xander audibly groaned. "Sorry if I took so long but I thought that I saw something hiding near some shelves, turned out to be a coat that someone had put behind some old paint cans. Accidently popped one open when I pulled it out too, doesn't look like anyone there is going to mind though."

"So we came all this way for nothing?" Xander stated as he put his hand to his head, Alkali nodding as he tried to mentally will the nosy reporter not to push it any further. "What about the blood trail though, and the light inside? Surely you saw something in there that could tell us where he went."

"I already told you that there's no one in there Xander," Alkali replied, his tone slightly more forceful to attempt to end the conversation. "Anyway the trail is about as cold as the wind, why don't we get out here before someone calls the cops on us. I think I remember seeing a diner just outside of here when we were in that rum runner's car, coffee's on me to try and warm you two up."

The promise of getting out of the freezing weather and a hot liquid to go into their bellies was enough to stop the conversation at that moment, but as the three of them began to walk back towards the road he could see Trinity glance over at him every so often. At this point there was nothing he could do or say about it that would help his case, he had to stick to the lie in order to investigate this Agent Poker more thoroughly and see what he wanted. In his mind he logged in everything that was said to him from the agent, from the fact that he was undercover merely posing to rob the gala all the way to him saying that he already had several leads on his case. Unfortunately he had been so vague about his plan to use the robbery as a means to infiltrate the Syndicate that the ferret couldn't make more in the way of connections at that moment.

Once the three of them had gotten to said diner and ordered their drinks, the black liquid thick enough to hold their spoons up briefly, Alkali stated that he would be heading back to his office in order to try and find anything related to the suspect they had seen. When Xander offered to help the ferret quickly told him that wouldn't be necessary and that he wouldn't let some reporter snoop around his files anyway. To his surprise Trinity merely nodded and stated she had to get back to the club as well, lamenting at the loss of pay for the night before leaving the still-full cup on the counter. It was something that a singer at a speakeasy would certainly say, but as Alkali watched her leave the words of the agent continued to echo in his head.

After taking a sip from his own mug Alkali quickly found the reason why the hybrid had left hers untouched, glancing over and seeing Xander make a similar face when he tried his. Despite that the two continued to talk for about half an hour before the ferret decided to head back to his place. There was another round of protest from the dragon who once more offered up his place for them to crash again, but at the very least he needed a drink after everything that happened tonight. The two left separately and Alkali hailed a cab, the night still early enough that it didn't take long before he was watching the streetlights streak past the frost covered window like well-coordinated fireflies.

The trip back to his place only took about fifteen minutes and when Alkali paid the fare and stepped outside his mind was still no closer to unraveling the details of this case. It was as if everything was tangled up like a ball of Christmas lights and every time he found a loose strand someone would come along and mix it all up again. He still wondered if it wasn't too late to potentially back out of this whole deal altogether, or at least make sure he distanced himself from the FBI on this case. The last thing he needed was someone thinking that he worked with them as it would not only ruin his reputation but also set him up as a target for criminal organizations such as the Kage Syndicate.

As he went up the stairs towards his floor Alkali also realized that other than the place that they were going to meet Poker had not specified a time for their meeting. He sighed slightly when he wondered if he was going to have to wait long for this rendezvous to happen, or if there was going to be some sort of call first. Since he was an undercover agent it was unlikely he could just call the branch office of the FBI and ask for him either, they would likely say that either he didn't exist or he was away on business since he was in the middle of an undercover operation. That meant the only thing he could do was wait, which was going to be made easier once he had a drink in his hand and a record playing in the warmth of his office.

When Alkali finally got up to his floor however he had to quickly put his daydreaming on hold upon discovering his lights were off. He always kept them on while he was away and as he slowly got closer he could see that his door was slightly ajar as well. Had someone figured out that he was talking to the feds, or had Trinity actually seen him talking with Poker and the Syndicate was about to get involved? Maybe Poker had decided to head right to his place after he was done in the warehouse, which given the time he had spent in the diner would have allowed the agent to get to his office before him. In any of the many scenarios that he had running through his mind he knew most of them didn't end well for him as he reached into his coat and pulled out his firearm.

The detective could feel his heart pounding in his chest as went over to the doorframe and tried to peak in, unable to see anything in the darkness of his office from the tiny crack. He grimaced inwardly when he used the muzzle of his firearm to slowly push open the door and heard the rusty hinges squeak in protest from years of neglect. While it helped him to hear if anyone was trying to come into his office it also did the same to anyone that happened to be inside as well. The hallway from the light spilled into the office as he continued to open the door until there was enough room for him to slip inside, leaving it that way so he could see while anyone that would attack him had to contend with the brightness that came in.

But as the blood continued to pulse through his body so loudly he could hear it in his ears Alkali didn't see any movement come from the shadows of his somewhat small office. There was no one here, at least no one in any obvious ambush to try and end his life. As he slowly stepped inside however he began to feel the unmistakable presence of someone that at the very least had been in his domicile. He had spent so many hours looking at every inch, every detail, of his office that he noticed when there was something slightly off about anything inside.

Alkali quickly made mental notes about anything he felt had been moved or disturbed as he made his way over to his desk, only to stop dead in his tracks when he got around to the back of it. He had already noticed his chair had been pushed off to one side but when he looked down at the carpet he saw why; a body had been sprawled out behind the desk that was illuminated only by the faint glow of the street lamps outside of his building. Even before he looked for identification the unmistakeable black fur and red pattern around the wolf's eye told him who this person was, the lupine having one additional red line across his neck given to him by someone else that dribbled with a similarly colored liquid. The gun that Alkali was holding hung limply from his hand as he saw the glint of light from the door reflect on the pool of blood that slowly gathered behind the head of the FBI agent he had just talked to almost an hour ago.

Agent Poker Wolf was dead in his office.

Almost immediately a shot of adrenaline better than any coffee hit the ferret's system and his analytical mind began to put the pieces together of what happened. Poker had come to his office in order to tell him more about the case he had been working on, and whether he had been followed or someone was watching his office the murderer came in and dispatched him. As Alkali looked over on his desk he could see that his phone was off the hook, a number of papers were spread about, and a glass that was sitting next to his tequila bottle had been knocked over to spill what contents remained onto the cheap wood. It seemed as though there was a struggle that happened here prior to Poker's death, and as he examined the lupine's head more closely he noted that in addition to his throat being slit there was a bloody wound on the back of his head.

Alkali quickly patted down the dead agent to see if he had anything of note in his pockets and found his gun and wallet, though the latter was different than the one that carried his badge. When he opened it up he saw an identification card with the wolf's picture on it but a different name that was likely his criminal alias. There was nothing else there that would help him though and the ferret quickly put everything back before quickly going into his living area to make sure no one was hiding there. At this point worrying about trace evidence was a moot point; finding the body in his office would already point everything in his direction even if he didn't have a motive for killing him.

When it was clear that there was no one else in the office apartment Alkali bit his lip as he went back to where the body laid, and continued to see the blue eyes of the wolf staring up at him as though in accusation. Part of him wanted to drink from that tequila bottle on his desk until he passed out but getting drunk would only add to his problems at this point. A flurry of ideas ran through his mind on how to handle the situation that ranged from calling the FBI to try and explain to dumping the body, with none of them having a good outcome that he could see. When he went back into his office though he quickly gathered that he wouldn't have the chance to do any of those things as the soft white glow on his windows became punctuated by flashing blue and red lights.

"That's an uncanny response time," Alkali muttered to himself as he carefully glanced out the window to see two black and whites parked outside the front of his building. Even if someone in the neighboring rooms had heard the scuffle between Poker and his attacker it would have been dumb luck to have one show up this quick, much less two. "This is starting to smell like a frame job…"

It made sense, Alkali thought to himself as he went over and locked the door to his office to buy himself a little more time. If someone from the Kage Syndicate had figured out that Poker was a fed, or even if they just thought that he was actually robbing the gala, and followed him to Alkali's office they could kill two birds with one stone. No… it had to be they found out he was a fed, the ferret corrected himself, otherwise they would have just dumped him in the harbor and that would have been it. Framing him for the murder ends the investigation, especially if a particularly influential criminal organization greased the wheels of justice to make sure he went down for it.

Alkali looked at his pocket watch and guessed that it had been about three minutes since the cop cars pulled up, which meant he likely had less then ten before they came in and broke down the door depending on the information they had. The ferret had no intention of being there when they did and pulled open his window, snow swirling in as cold cascaded into the normally warm office. As he started to climb over the sill to hop onto the fire escape he looked back at the body and wondered if it was cold, which was unlikely if he had just gotten there. In the back of his mind his investigative instincts wondered just how long Poker had been in his office before he had been attacked, as well as how he managed to get past his locked door in the first place.

The pause he had taken for his introspection had cost him time though as Alkali looked up upon hearing voices on the other side of his office door. Without another second to lose he got onto the rickety fire escape and closed the window behind him, hoping that he could get away without being seen. It wouldn't be strange for him to be out all night on a case and that would hopefully give him time to find more information on Poker's killer before the police put out a warrant on him for questioning. As he grabbed the sides of the railings to head down the metal stairs he could hear the sound of wood splintering and imagined that the officers had already kicked down his door, causing him to frown when he thought of how much it would cost to get that fixed.

Once he had gotten away from his own windows Alkali looked up to see the lights in his office turn on, the body that lay hidden behind his desk mere seconds away from being discovered. The cold iron bit against his exposed palms as he tried to quickly but carefully make his way down the icy fire escape to the street below. Just a floor before he reached freedom, he thought to himself as he got to the last platform, and when he got to the ladder he tried to pull the clasp to drop it so he could go down to the street. The combination of rust and ice made it hard to undo however and the ferret found himself pushing with all his strength until finally the clasp released.

Unfortunately Alkali had been so focused on getting it that he forgot to retain his hold on the ladder, and with nothing to keep it up it slid all the way down before it stopped with a loud crash. Almost immediately the ferret looked over where the cop cars were parked and saw that a husky-racoon man that had been sitting there was staring back at him, and after giving the officer a sheepish grin he tried to scramble down the ladder as quickly as possible. The rungs were just as icy as the rest of the fire escape though and after he felt his foot slip Alkali remained suspended in mid-air briefly before he landed flat on his back. The snow bank he had fallen into kicked the frozen stuff up into the air and blanketed his fall, but by the time he had managed to get the fur on his face cleaned off so that he could see he found himself staring down the barrel of a gun.

"Hands in the air!" the huscoon cop shouted, prompting Alkali to immediately comply before he was turned around and felt his arms get yanked behind his back and put into cuffs. It wasn't long after that he found himself yanked back up to his feet and heard the hybrid report in that they had the suspect in custody. It took all his power not to grit his teeth when he realized that he had just been caught in what looked like an attempt to flee the scene of the crime as he was pushed into the back seat of the car before the door was slammed shut.

Alkali pressed his head against the glass window as he attempted to get more comfortable in his restrained state as he saw several more emergency vehicles arrive on the scene. It was like they were forcing him to watch as teams came in to collect evidence from his office. He couldn't help but groan as he watched them take the tequila bottle in an evidence back outside along with a number of his other personal effects, wishing that he had at least taken one drink before they would likely take it out behind the police station and dump it, or possibly have it for themselves. The one thing that he found himself unable to watch and turned his head away was when the stretcher came out with the body bag on it, the FBI agent no doubt inside.

After several long and grueling hours the police officer that had originally arrested him got in his car and took off, taking the private eye down to the station to be booked like so many others he had investigated before.

Chapter Four – By the Book

The processing didn't take as long as Alkali had expected, after fingerprinting and his mugshot he had been taken to the back of the police station where they had the interrogation rooms. Despite his years as a private investigator he rarely saw either side of them, especially since most of his interviews took place in seedy back alleys or smoke-filled bar rooms. As he looked around the décor wasn't much different than those places, except for the large mirror that showed his reflection and the steel table that was bolted to the floor. Once he was seated in one of the extremely uncomfortable chairs the cuffs that had been attached to his wrists were taken off, allowing the ferret to rub his wrists while the skunk that had taken them off circled around to the other side of the table.

"My name is Detective Firr," the skunk introduced himself as he sat down on the other side of the table and opened the bright blue folder that he had carried in with him. "It seems that you've always just been on the right side of the law despite your profession, though the company you keep certainly doesn't join you in that regard. Quite the leap over to the dark side committing murder, especially to an FBI agent."

So he really was an FBI agent, Alkali thought to himself before looking up at Firr. "That's why this whole thing is one big misunderstanding," Alkali replied as he put his hands against his head. "Why on earth would I kill someone in my own office, and someone I just met no less! All I was doing was following a case that had been given to me where someone thought that he was going to rob a charity gala."

"Ah yes, I read that in your initial booking statement," Firr replied as he leaned back in the chair, kicking his feet up onto the table while moving the papers in the folder around. "You were hired by a singer, whom you won't identify, in a speakeasy, which you won't reveal, becaase she thought a crime might be committed by Agent Wolf, who was undercover on an operation that you claim you know nothing about." Even though Alkali nodded in affirmation he could see that the skunk wasn't buying it just by the look that was given to him. "I see… is there any more information that you don't want to tell me?"

"Look, I realize that it seems I'm being uncooperative but there's really not much more that I can say about it," Alkali practically pleaded. "All you have to do is call up the FBI and have them tell you what he was working on, and then you'll see there's no reason for me to have gotten involved. Not to mention that you didn't find a knife on me and there was none at the crime scene, so-"

There was a loud bang as Firr took something he had been hiding and tossed it on the table, Alkali's eyes widening when he saw a black metal blade glimmer in the light. There was a small line of red on the edge of it and the ferret had a decent guess on what that probably was as the skunk leaned forward. "We found that in the locked drawer at the bottom of your desk," Firr explained. "I guess you figured since you weren't stashing your illegal booze there that it would hold your murder weapon instead?"

"That's… that's not mine!" Alkali exclaimed back, though he knew how it sounded even as the words left his muzzle he knew how ridiculous they sounded. It was the same thing he had heard dozens of times from those that he had caught, some red handed while in the middle of the act, and it rang just as hollow then as it did now. "I… I just… I need…"

Suddenly the door opened with such intensity that it caused a gust of wind to ruffle the fur of the two as a badger in a suit came in and slammed a briefcase against the table. "What my client needs is some alone time with his counsel," the badger said as he held out his card to the surprised detective. "Boozy Badger, Attorney at Law, now I do hope that you ascertained the rights of my client before you decided to ambush him with these potentially frivolous evidentiary exclamations?"

"Frivolous!?" Firr practically shouted as he got up, nearly knocking the chair behind him. "I have your client leaving the scene of the crime, the murder weapon locked in his desk, and a dead FBI agent in his office!"

"Well you did get one thing right," Boozy said as he picked up the chair and sat down in it. "you do have a dead FBI agent, everything else you just said is not only circumstantial but potentially inflammatory as well! Now why don't you make good on being a bother to my client and get us a couple cups of what your department might consider coffee."

"Why… you… I…" it was clear to Alkali that the lawyer had flustered the officer, the big tail of the skunk twitching as he slowly backed out of the interrogation room while the two watched him. "Oh, I'll get you two your coffees alright… you just wait, I'll make sure to get you all the coffee you could want. And cream… and sugar…"

The skunk could still be heard talking even after he had closed the door, which prompted the badger to shake his head. "Something not right with that boy," Boozy said before he went and opened his case. "So, killed an FBI agent, definitely one of the top crimes a client of mine has done."

"But I DIDN'T KILL HIM!" Alkali replied, practically sputtering his words as he nearly face-planted his head into the table.

"Now now, I'm your lawyer, you don't need to lie to me," Boozy said as he took out a cigar and lit it. "So if you want this thing to just go away I know a judge that owes me a few favors, but I hope you put some money away in your rainy day top hat because the bribes are going to get expensive quick. Otherwise you can take this to the courts and I could try to fabricate some doubt, which is cheaper but more of a roll of the dice."

"How are you a lawyer?!" Alkali exclaimed loudly. "I'm innocent!"

"Really?" Boozy replied, giving the ferret a look before shrugging his shoulders. "Well innocent or not the last thing the department wants is an open murder on their books, especially that of an FBI agent. If they don't serve up a sacrifice then they're going to come down on this city like a plague of locusts, and that's not good for anybody. Now if you're strapped for cash I represent a lot of moonshiners that can help move you out of the city, you just say the word and I know a guy that can fake your death real easy."

Alkali couldn't believe what he was hearing; Boozy had helped him out of some rough scrapes where he had been at the wrong place at the wrong time before, but never had he heard the badger give him such dire solutions to the problem at hand. He knew deep down though that he was right and that the police weren't going to give him much room to wiggle when it came to this case. They needed to close it fast before they lost jurisdiction to the feds and if they did then all manner of criminal activity could be exposed. It was no secret that a number of officers were on the take, whether paid to look the other way or personally involved there would be quite a few that would lose their jobs at minimum if a wide-scale investigation took place.

After about ten minutes Alkali told Boozy that he needed to think about what was being told to him, the lawyer nodding and informing him not to take any more interviews until he had made up his mind on his next step. Once the badger left the skunk detective came in with several cups of coffee only to be told they were not needed, which caused Firr's eye to twitch slightly before he sat down in the vacant seat. Alkali quickly told the officer that he wasn't going to take any more questions and Boozy quickly backed him up in saying that he needed some rest, which prompted the skunk to throw his hands up and toss the cups behind him before saying fine. A minute later the cuffs were back on Alkali's wrists and he was led through the police department to holding, feeling the eyes of the others in the station staring at him in judgement as he passed by them.

Since public holding had the potential of the private investigator meeting friends or enemies of his it was opted that he went to one of the two single holding cells near the back. This space was mostly reserved for drunks and those that were just being held overnight but for Alkali they were making an exception as they led him into the first open one in the room. There was a chill in the air and the ferret could hear wind whistling through the cracks in the deteriorated concrete as he was uncuffed once inside and given a bedroll and pillow. The entire time he remained quiet until the door slammed closed and he was plunged into darkness with the only light coming from a small viewing hole in the main door.

A dead FBI agent and he was the main suspect, Alkali thought with a sigh as he tossed the thin padding on the metal bench and sat down on top of it. Everything on his person had been confiscated so he couldn't even write down his thoughts as he tried to think about who could have put him in this position. His first and main thought was the Kage Syndicate, particularly Trinity, who had shot Poker the same night. But if they had found out he was an FBI agent then it was unlikely that they would kill him the more he thought about it, if they had found that out they would have just fed him false information and embarrassed him.

The ferret pressed the back of his head against the wall as the primary motive for killing the agent alluded him like a shadow at the corner of his vision. Any time he thought he might have one some piece of logic came in and made it more unlikely. It was no wonder that the police were just going to have him be the one that would be the suspect, whatever story they would concoct for him to be the killer would be just as outlandish as anything that he had thought of so far. Either way there was nothing he could do at the moment except contemplate Boozy's solutions and pick the one that would be the least likely to put him in prison for the rest of his life.

 With no clock in the room and his pocket watch taken from him there was no way for Alkali to know what time it was in the windowless room, and just as he was about to consider actually laying down for the night to attempt sleep the outside door to the station opened again. At first they thought that skunk officer was about to try and have another run at him but as he looked over he saw that it was two of the bigger guys with each one holding the arm of someone that appeared to be unconscious. "This is the third one tonight," the bull officer said as they dragged the guy between them along until they got to the next cell where the lizardman officer opened it. "I know that we can't track down where every drunk came from but if we let this go any more we're going to have a bunch of frozen vagrants out on the street."

"Look, we just do what we're told," the lizardman said as they walked in, deposited the one between them, and walked back out. "As soon as he thaws out and sobers up we'll kick him to the curb with the others. Now come on, I heard Ronald brought his chicken soup in today and I'm freezing to my bones."

The two continued to chat with one another before they left, leaving Alkali in the dark once more with his thoughts. If only he could get to that gin joint and talk to Trinity, at the very least he could try to set the record straight and figure out what was going on. This case felt like a puzzle with half the pieces thrown out, and before he had a chance to find them someone put a sheet over the whole thing and told him to stop. His mind wouldn't let him stop though, not until he got to the truth of what happened.

Just then Alkali's ears perked up as he heard a low chuckle come from the cell next to him, the one where they had put the drunk in minutes before. "Sometimes it's just too easy," the voice said in the darkness as he heard more movement. "Just to make sure, you're Detective Alkali Bismuth?"

"So I've been told," Alkali replied cautiously. "Why?"

"Name's Serathin," the voice called back, Alkali seeing a blue-scaled hand reach over that he shook after a few seconds. "Someone is paying me a lot of money to make sure that you're not locked up, so just sit right there and do what I say so that we don't get shot."

"You're breaking me out?" Alkali asked, hearing the other man merely let out a noise of affirmation. "Look, I haven't even considered what Boozy is asking of me yet, so I-"

"Oh, this isn't coming from your lawyer," Serathin stated. "You've attracted the attention of someone from much higher in the food chain, and as such you will be expected to come to his summons. Now stop asking me things, I just slipped the string off my tooth and if I swallow this then we're both going to be in trouble."

Though Alkali's inquisitive nature wanted to know more about what was happening he stayed quiet, and as he went up to the bars to try and see what was happening he could hear a series of gagging and choking noises. The ferret's eyes looked around and saw the reflection of the person in the other cell just as they slowly pulled a string out from their throat until something on the end of it came out as well. Serathin took a deep breath before opening the saliva-soaked leather holder and pulled out a few pieces of thin metal, then reached through the bars and pushed them into the lock. Within a matter of seconds there was a loud click and the cell door slowly opened, then closed before he moved over to his.

Now that the two were much closer he could see that this guy was a hybrid of wolf and dragon, though he also had a pair of saberteeth that hung past his lip as he picked the door. Alkali didn't have long to look the hybrid over before his freedom was secured as well. But that was only the first obstacle in their path, they were still in the middle of a police station filled with cops. Since it was the middle of the night there were only a few on duty though, but still the sabrewolf told Alkali to wait as he looked out the viewing window. An increasing sense of nervousness filled the ferret but as he looked out as well he suddenly saw several officers run past the door on their way towards the motor pool.

"Had a friend call in an officer down and shots fired with a radio that they stole from this dispatch a few weeks ago," Serathin explained as he opened the door and poked his head out. "I doubt anyone is going to stick around on a call like that so we have a few minutes to get out of here before they realize it's a fake."

Alkali nodded and followed his fellow escapee down the corridor and into the station proper. Just as the hybrid had said there was no one left in the office, all of them speeding out into the cold night air to aid a cop that didn't exist. Though the ferret wanted nothing more to get out of there as the two passed the evidence locker he tapped on Serathin's shoulder and asked if they could go in and get his things out. From the frown on the scaled muzzle of the hybrid's face he was not enthused about the idea, but when he insisted it would only take a minute he sighed and pulled out his lockpick set once again. This guy was fast, Alkali thought to himself as he watched the draconic sabrewolf once more move the instruments inside the lock until it turned and clicked open.

The two carefully poked their heads inside and saw that the room was empty, then after another round of lockpicking Alkali found himself surrounded by evidence confiscated by the police. As the sabrewolf helped himself to a stack of money that had likely been taken from a gambling den raid he looked for his own personal effects. He knew that they had to be somewhere in the most recent section of the log and it didn't take him long before he found the box with his name on it. As he pulled it from the shelf it caught the interest of Serathin who moved over and watched as he broke the evidence tape and opened the lid.

"Here we are…" Alkali said as he pulled the pocket watch out and ripped the plastic bag from it, then put it back in his coat. "Alright, what else do we have here…"

"Whoa, this is some good stuff," Serathin said as he reached in while Alkali grabbed for his gun and pulled out the bottle of tequila. "Not much of a tequila drinker myself but I can tell you have some good taste. This is from before prohibition, right?"

"Yeah, saved a few before everything got smashed in the first round of raids," Alkali said as he took his gun out and removed the evidence tag from that. "Why don't we take it with us and we can share a drink as my thanks for getting me out of this."

"Sounds like a plan to me," Serathin said as he pulled the bottle out of the plastic and set it on the table before looking back into the box while Alkali grabbed the holster from his weapon too. "Man, looks like they took your entire office and put it in here, you know you can't take it all right?"

"These two are fine for me," Alkali said as he felt the familiar weight of his gun press against his side, an almost comforting reassurance despite the insanity that was swirling around him. With the two items he wanted in hand he quickly put the cover back on and tried to make the tape look as intact as possible. "Let's put this back on the shelf, if we're lucky they won't even notice it's missing."

Serathin nodded and pulled the box towards him, and as he did both men stopped when they heard a loud crash. Alkali clutched at his chest as he looked down at the floor and saw the broken bottle of tequila surrounded by its liquid remains, and though he heard Serathin hiss through his teeth and apologize it was a distant echo in his ears. Not even seeing the dead body of the FBI agent compared to the anguish he felt as he looked down at the destroyed liquor while feeling his knees shake slightly. His tequila… his precious tequila…

Just as the room started to spin and his vision start to go black Serathin quickly snapped his fingers in front of his face. "Now is definitely not the time to cry over spilt tequila, now hold on…" Alkali watched as Serathin opened the box once more and dug around until he pulled out the knife, using the blade to free it from its plastic confines before going over and cutting a shrink-wrapped pallet that was in the corner before he pulled something out. "Here, give this a cuddle and let's get out of here."

Alkali looked down at the bottle that he was holding and saw that it was a vintage tequila that appeared to be store-brand as well, the anguish and despair he felt in his heart lifting as he practically nuzzled the bottle while they walked out of the evidence room and back into the police station. Just as they were about to leave through the back they could hear voices that came from the garage area that indicated the cops were starting to come back from the bogus call. By that point however they had already left the station and were heading down the street where Serathin had parked a car to drive them towards their next destination. As Alkali heard the alarm go off in the station just as they got out of hearing distance though part of him wondered if he had just jumped out of the frying pan and into the fire…

Serathin drove the two of them around for about half an hour before they finally arrived in an area on the other side of the city, the police radio inside of the hybrid's car squawking with news that the one responsible for the murder of an FBI agent had broken free of police custody. If he wasn't thought of doing it before they certainly did now, the ferret thought to himself with some chagrin. What he needed to do was find Poker's killer and clear his name, but at the moment he was more fixated on his current predicament as the car eventually reached the back parking lot of a building and stopped. As they got out of the car the two were met by a rather large rhino man in a tuxedo and at that time Alkali couldn't help but notice the club they had parked around the back of.

The upscale nightclub was called The Anthro Connoisseur, but everyone knew it by its nickname of Anthrocon. This was where the Kage Syndicate based their operations; everyone who did business with or was a part of the criminal organization hung out here and it was considered off-limits even to someone like him. At the very least the cops wouldn't dare to try and get him here, the only ones that went inside this building were those that were on the cockroach's payroll. Despite being an apparently invited guest Alkali couldn't help but feel a lump form in his stomach as he passed through the security doors and surrendered his sidearm before stepping inside.

As soon as he got on the other side of the threshold he was immediately awash in warmth and the sound of loud music. Alkali could see the alcoholic drinks flowing to the patrons that were gathered within and knew that for them there was no risk of being raided. A pink-scaled dragon bartender had a number of exposed liquor bottles that were similar to the one that he continued to hold and knew that they were all likely top-shelf draws from before prohibition. There wouldn't be any bathtub booze found in this establishment, not for someone as well connected as the one in charge.

Both Alkali and Serathin walked past the coyote and fox that were playing a smooth jazz ensemble for the crowd and made their way up a set of spiral stairs to the upper level. Once they had gotten to the second floor the music suddenly was hard to hear and things got eerily quiet. The fun and frivolity that was experienced downstairs was replaced by a strict air of business as men and women in suits talked to one another. This was how the upper echelons of such organizations were run, Alkali thought to himself, and as they went past the group and into a large office at the end of the room they saw the leader of it all behind an ornate mahogany desk with gold inlay.

"Seems you've got yourself in a spot of trouble my boy," the cockroach said as he stood up and put a bowler hat on his head, the two bodyguards moving with him as he went down to where the ferret and sabrewolf sat. "From my sources I'm told that you went ahead and stabbed an agent in your own office, not very smart. If you wanted to make the leap to serious crime you should have told me, someone with your skills could be so much more than a simple murderer."

"I think you and I both know that I was not involved in this killing Uncle Kage," Alkali replied, puffing up his chest slightly in an attempt to remain defiant despite the vibrations of terror that were coursing through his body. With one simple flick of his antennae the ferret would find himself full of lead, but the fact he remained on his own two feet gave him enough confidence that he hadn't been brought here just to be executed. "I also think you already knew that Agent Wolf was trying to bait you by pretending to the rob the charity gala this week, or am I wrong?"

A wry smile appeared on the face of the cockroach and we went over towards a small table where a crystalline decanter sat along with two glasses. "Would you care for a drink, I have a fine Riesling that I just had imported… or if you want I could pour you a glass from that bottle you're clutching for dear life," Alkali looked down at the bottle he had and realized that he had been holding onto it ever since he saw his own supply shattered on the ground, handing it to one of the guards who gave it a quick sip before nodding to Uncle Kage who began to pour it. "In any case you are correct that we had found out the identity of Agent Wolf after we heard word that someone was attempting to rob us, but instead of engaging we decided that we would let the scenario happen and play him for the fool."

"I knew it," Alkali said as he grabbed the glass from the cockroach, Serathin doing the same when one was presented to him. "So that means you didn't have him killed… but if it wasn't you, then who?"

"That is something we hoped bringing you in would answer," Uncle Kage replied. "A murder of an FBI agent is no good for anyone in this city, and we need to find out who it is before they decide to come down here and look for themselves. Now I've pulled a few strings and made sure that your escape is kept from the public as well as other police stations, and the one that does know of it has been instructed to keep it under wraps for their own sake. However… if you can't find the one who did it within forty-eight hours then the manhunt begins again and there will be no place where you can hide anywhere in this city, and if you try to leave the police have set up road blocks to prevent your premature departure."

Forty-eight hours… while it wasn't the first time for Alkali that he had been put on a clock like this it had never been for stakes as high as these. He knew that Uncle Kage had already spread his feelers out and made sure that there was no way that he would be able to escape the net that was placed for him. Either he would find Poker's killer in two days and the cockroach would be sure to send that person to the FBI, or he would be the one that was sent up the frozen river. The two continued to talk for a while during their drink and when Uncle Kage asked Alkali's next step in the investigation would be he found it hard to think of an answer on what to do other then go to the safehouse and find those files Poker had.

"Why don't you enjoy our hospitality for the night and start fresh in the morning," Uncle Kage suggested. "You've been through quite the ordeal and I think that a little rest might do you some good, the safehouse you mentioned isn't going anywhere. The clock is still ticking though so do make sure that you don't sleep in."

Once more Alkali couldn't help but feel that lump in his throat return, though the burn of the tequila helped to smooth over the rough edges that he had been having that night. Since he doubted he could sleep at his own place with it being a crime scene and not wanting to attract attention at a hotel he decided to take the crime boss up on his offer. He gave Serathin another thanks for helping him escape in the first place and then followed one of the bouncers to another area of the club that had a number of rooms. While the ferret doubted that any of them were for sleeping he wasn't going to let the opportunity pass him by and practically collapsed on the soft sheets, the last thought in his mind was the hope that tomorrow he would open his eyes and find out that it was all a bad dream.

Chapter Five – The Investigation Begins

The next morning Alkali awoke to a knock at the door, and after wiping the drool off of his face fur and checking the time on his watch he went over to answer it. While he expected it to be Uncle Kage he found instead that it was one of the guards that informed him that there was a car waiting to take him wherever he needed to go and that there was also breakfast waiting. Despite the generosity as he followed the large alligator man down to a room that was set up as a private dining area he couldn't help but feel that it was more like a last meal. His time wasn't quite up though, with it being eight in the morning he still had forty hours to find the murderer and clear his name.

While he sat and ate Alkali asked the alligator that continued to accompany him if he could get a pen and notepad. It was one of things that he hadn't grabbed from the box and as he wrote down all the information that he could remember on the case he remembered that there was actually two places he could go in order to find information on what Poker was doing and who may want him dead. The first place was the Foxhole, which was where he had attempted to recruit people for the fake heist, and then there was also the warehouse where he first met the wolf. Before that though he needed to get a few more people on his side to help with investigating, especially since he was up against a very hard wall with the time crunch.

When he was finished with breakfast the bodyguard asked if there was anything else he needed, to which Alkali replied that he needed to use the telephone. After making a few calls the ferret went out to the car that was waiting for him and gave him the address of the Foxhole, which is where he had told the others to meet him there. So far he had managed to get Xander and Draggor to respond to his summons as well as the owner of the establishment, and though he didn't know Trinity's number the fox assured him that he could get a hold of her. Four people weren't bad to have on his side to figure this out and for good measure he had also asked Uncle Kage to contact the cat burglar that had broken him out and see if he was up for another job.

As Alkali was driven through the city towards his destination he couldn't help but be surprised at how lively everything looked during the day. With most of his work being done in the night it was hard for him to find time to enjoy being out when the sun was up and despite it still being very cold out there were quite a few people moving about on their way to work or some other destination. Every so often he would catch a glance of someone who attempted to look into the windows of the fancy car he was in, but with the tinted windows it was unlikely anyone would recognize him. Not only that but as Uncle Kage had promised it appeared nothing had been leaked to the news of his arrest or the dead FBI agent, which means that he could operate through most of the city without too much worry of being apprehended.

It was still better not to press his luck though and until Alkali got to the speakeasy he kept his head down in the car. Eventually he got to where he needed to go and the driver wished him luck as he stepped outside into the brisk morning air. Even though the entire street looked relatively dead he knew that everyone waited for him inside, stepping through the front door that he found unlocked. When he got to the bar he saw that everyone he had asked for was there, including Trinity who just looked at him with a curious glance.

"You know, I didn't believe it for a second when they said that you stabbed an FBI agent," Draggor stated first as they went over and hugged the ferret with Xander right behind. "Xander over here was writing up his next article though about the murder."

"I was not!" the dragon retorted quickly, the others in the room chuckling a bit as Xander blushed slightly. "But I am happy to hear that you are being given a chance to catch the guy that framed you, how much time do you have left?"

"Not enough," Alkali quickly stated as he motioned for the two to go back to their seats. "The reason I asked you all here was because I need you in order to try and solve this case within the time frame given to me. I figure with a reporter, a criminal liaison, a speakeasy owner, a sneak thief, and a singer we can reach out and try to find who might have wanted Poker dead or to frame me.”

“I know that he had contacted quite a few people through my place and paid me handsomely to do so,” Zen said with a grin. “Since I don’t want to be known as the bar that led to the death of an FBI agent I’ll see what I can scrounge up on his past contacts with the help of Trinity.”

“Serathin and I will hit up the criminal connections,” Draggor exclaimed, the sabrewolf nodding in response. “Maybe someone besides the Kage Syndicate thought they could make a name for themselves or get in their good graces by taking out a potential thief. It would help though if we had a few leads, if we try and shake down everyone in the city it’s going to take months, not days.”

“That’s what Xander and I are about to do,” Alkali stated, which caused the dragon to look up. “We’re going to go back to the warehouse where I first met Agent Poker and hope that his files are still there. If he had managed to recruit serious robbers and they found out that it was a scam they might have just killed him wherever they found him and ended their grudge there.”

The others nodded and began to get to work, but before Alkali and Xander went out to the warehouse the ferret found Trinity getting his attention. She motioned for him to follow her to the back of the speakeasy where her dressing room was and the ferret began to feel slightly nervous at the sudden isolation. “Hey there Momma T,” Alkali said, noting the furrows on her forehead and the anger present on her muzzle. “What’s wrong?”

“You know very well what’s wrong,” Trinity said as the scowl deepened on her face. “I asked you if you made contact with Agent Wolf and you told me that there was no one there!” She sighed and sat down in her chair, looking down at the wood of the vanity while putting her hands on her head. “If you had just informed me of what was going on then you probably wouldn't be in this scenario right now…"

For a few seconds Alkali wasn't sure why the wolf-dog was taking this so hard, but then a lightning bolt of realization hit him that caused his eyes to widen in surprise. "Sorry, Agent Poker thought that you might have been working for the Kage Syndicate," the ferret said as she looked back up at him. "I'm sure if he knew that you were actually an agent yourself he would have told you about his operation."

The grimace on Trinity's face evaporated slightly as she looked up with a small grin that played at the edge of her muzzle. "Well, it appears that you've finally caught up," Trinity said as she stood up. "I'm actually ATF, and we had no idea that there were any FBI ops that were going on in this location. Of course given Agent Wolf had not identified himself in that back alley after pulling a gun on him I can only guess that our departments once more failed to talk to one another."

Two government agents operating within the same gin joint in the city; no doubt both were targeting the Kage Syndicate and it seemed they thought that the Foxhole was the place to be when it came to such a thing. Perhaps one had drawn the other there, but in either case at the moment it was a moot point and only served to further cross Trinity off of his list as a potential suspect. "I can assume that you will not divulge the details of my work since my operation is still intact," Trinity continued on. "Last thing you need is more charges being added to that file of yours."

"Well, of course I won't say anything," Alkali quickly replied. "But can't you just tell the FBI that I didn't kill Poker and get me off this hook?"

"I would love to help you out, but I'm afraid I can't blow my op just because a pretty face came up and asked me nicely," Trinity explained. "In all seriousness though even if I did vouch for you not only would I reveal myself but it would also probably make little difference in the long run considering the reach of the Syndicate. The only thing I can suggest to you is that you find this killer before that forty-eight hours is up, or before the killer finds you."

The ice-cold words of the one that called herself Momma T struck Alkali like a knife in his chest. He hadn't thought about it before but if the killer realized that he was being given the opportunity to clear his name it was possible that they would come after him to make sure it didn't happen. While it wouldn't wrap the case up in a neat little bow like they would want it would stop him from being able to investigate. For the moment he would just have to hope that he could stay one step ahead of them, or that they wouldn't find out that he was on to them until the moment he could strike.

With the air cleared between him and the wolf-dog Alkali once more joined up with Xander in order to go to the warehouse near the docks and find the evidence the agent had compiled. Zen and Trinity would remain at the Foxhole in order to put together a list of people that Poker met with while the remaining two waited to see what the detective and reporter might find to aid them in their search. The ferret and dragon made their way out of the speakeasy and back to where the driver was parked, only to find that the car he had been given to get down there was gone. It appeared that since he was away from the nightclub Kage's generosity had run dry, which meant they needed another way to get to where they needed to go.

As Xander mused if it was safe to take a cab with Alkali's status as a fugitive still potentially lingering the ferret looked back and saw the alley that he had chased Poker down initially. Though it was empty at the moment it hadn't been the night before, and that gave the detective an idea as he went back into the bar and got Zen's attention. "Hey, do you have the number of that bootlegger driver that makes deliveries to you?" Alkali asked, the fox nodding his head before asking him why. "We're going to need a lift…"

About an hour and a half later Xander and Alkali were once again in the back of the bouncing truck with Pandez driving them to their destination. Though it had taken a little coaxing to get the bootlegger to come out and chauffer them to where they needed to go the promise that he was helping out the Kage Syndicate greased the wheels to get him back into the city. "You think he would let us sit in the front this time," Xander muttered after a particularly large bump caused both of them to fly up into the air slightly.

"Sorry, don't want anyone to see me driving you two around," Pandez replied through the window between the cab and back. "Already get enough heat as it is with the deliveries I make, last thing I need is to get this bad boy impounded on a personal errand."

"That's great and all, but…" Alkali trailed off slightly as he looked around the empty back of the truck. "There's nothing even in here that you could get in trouble for!"

"Well you two are there now, so there's that," Pandez retorted.

Xander just rolled their eyes and tried to hold onto the side of the truck to prevent themselves from being bounced around anymore than they already had been. "You're lucky that this is going to make one heck of a story," the dragon said as they looked over at the ferret who also was attempting to brace himself. "I better be the first that breaks this."

"Hey, as long as you stick to the story that they're giving you it's practically exclusive," Alkali replied. "Also, I doubt that they're going to let me go back to the nightclub for another night, so until this whole thing blows over and my place is no longer a crime scene could I crash at your place?"

Xander smirked slightly at that and caused Alkali to do the same. "I suppose the last thing I want to do is have the ferret freeze to death out in the cold," Xander stated. "Of course I'm going to expect you to do a few things for me, and I'm not just talking about simple chores."

"Ah hey, I hate to break up the lovey-dovey that's going on back there but I think we might have a problem," Pandez interrupted, causing both of them to look up at the panda as he glanced back at them. "You said that this place you want me to take you to is near the back of the docks, right?"

"Yeah," Alkali said, concern rising inside of him as he shuffled himself forward towards the window. "Why?"

"There's quite the dark cloud that's hanging over that area," Pandez stated as he pointed at his windshield when Alkali got his head up to look out. "And I don't mean that metaphorically either."

The ferret's eyes grew wide and he could feel his jaw drop when he saw the column of black smoke that had risen up from the dockyards. Though it was hard to tell from this distance it appeared to be in the general area of where Poker's safehouse was, but secretly Alkali hoped that it happened to be some other building that was causing such an effect. A few minutes later however the three pulled up to the side alley just in front of the smoldering remains of the building that he had been in last night. Even though there was only a firetruck that was nearby Pandez told them to quickly hop out before driving his bootlegger special towards the entrance of the dockyard in case any police joined in the investigation.

Alkali and Xander could only stare on at the remains of the warehouse, which had been reduced to a framework of charred beams and smoldering metal. It appeared that the fire itself had been put out quite some time ago with one team left behind to make sure there were no flare-ups. Alkali told the dragon to go and make use of his reporter credentials to try and see if he could get any information on what caused the fire while he attempted to get the files themselves. It was a long shot that anything could have survived the blaze but with his life on the line he was sure going to try as he crept towards the husk of a room that had been the shipping office.

Once he had gotten into position he waited until he saw Xander engage with one of the firemen, and as soon as the focus on was on the dragon he crept inside while trying not to make any noise. As he stepped over what was left of the window sill he could see the others had taken notice of the reporter on scene and had moved over to see if they could put in their ten cents worth, which was just fine for the ferret as his feet stepped on burned remains that crunched underneath his shoes. He was glad he hadn't decided to change into a different pair as he saw them get covered with soot and grimy water that was still stagnant on the concrete floor. When he looked around the office though it was hard for him to determine where the grate was that contained all of the agent's files in it even was as he poked around.

For a few minutes Alkali tried to push away some debris that used to be shelves but all he found underneath was blackened concrete that caused his heart to sink. This was the only major lead that they had on the real criminals that were working with Poker, and even if he could find the grate it was unlikely that anything had survived the fire or the subsequent putting out. He also knew that Xander would probably not be able to stall them for long, yet the detective continued to try and figure out where the information could possibly be within the smoldering remains. When nothing else seemed to work he stopped and took a deep breath, closing his eyes to try and remember the night before and get a decent layout of the office.

After a few minutes Alkali found that the mental reconstruction didn't work for him but he did hear something that caused his ears to twitch. His eyes snapped open when he realized that the sound which captured his attention was water trickling down a drain, and with that as his only cue he tried to follow it as best he could. Soon the ferret's hands were covered in black soot as he moved aside a piece of ceiling that had collapsed into the office and carefully scraped away the shards of glass beneath to reveal the metal grate beneath. For a brief second Alkali wondered if the fire might have fused the metal or that this was the wrong one, but that jolt to his nerves quickly settled when it popped free and allowed him to stick his hand inside.

Alkali stuck his tongue out in slight disgust at the slimy nature of the tunnel he was pushing his hand through but eventually his fingers hit solid paper. The detective very carefully extracted the files as best he could and shook the gunk off of them before putting them in his coat, then as a second thought he reached back in until he found the FBI badge as well. When he flipped the leather wallet open he saw that the paper ID had been completely destroyed but the metal shield was still intact as he put it in his pocket as well. With everything he could find tucked away he stood up, and as soon as he did he heard someone shout in his direction that caused him to look back and see one of the firefighters coming towards him at a healthy clip.

"What do you think you're doing here?!" the angry cheetah said as he hopped over several destroyed walls to come up to him. "This place is highly unstable!"

"Oh, sorry about that, uh, Douglas," Alkali replied, quickly taking a look at the nameplate on the cheetah's uniform before continuing on. "I'm just, you know, I'm with them!"

The firefighter turned his head just in time to see Xander coming towards them while waving a hand in the air. "Hey, there you are!" Xander said, quickly queueing in on the confrontation and giving the cheetah a smile. "I deeply apologize for him, he's in training as my new photographer and doesn't quite know the ropes."

"Your… photographer…" Douglas replied as he glanced over at Alkali, then back to Xander. "Where's his camera?"

"Well now you see just how much work we have to do with him!" Xander exclaimed, not missing a beat as they grabbed Alkali by the arm and began to lead him away from the burned-out warehouse. "What did I tell you, in order to take pictures you have to have a camera! I can't believe you forgot it again!"

"Ohhh, is that what that was you were pointing at?" Alkali replied, trying not to look back to see if they were being followed as they began to move at an increasingly healthy pace away. "I just thought that you were trying to show me the equipment that you had! Man, I'd lose my head if it wasn't attached."

The back and forth continued for a few more moments before Xander turned back after they had gotten past a few old shipping containers. "Well, either they bought it or don't care enough to give chase," the dragon exclaimed, which caused them both to breathe a sigh of relief. "Did you manage to find anything?"

"At least what's left of it," Alkali replied as he opened his coat to show the dirty files. "Let's bring them back to Zen's place and see if we can make anything out of it. Oh, did you find out anything about the fire?"

"Yeah, the guy says that they received the call at about three-thirty in the morning," Xander said while they walked back to Pandez and the car. "By that point the fire had completely engulfed the entire warehouse and they said that it took quite a long time for them to put it out. While they can't give an official statement on it yet they said that it probably was arson and that some sort of accelerant was used."

Alkali just nodded in response; part of the ferret knew that was going to be the case, especially with the convenient timing that it burned down. He put the event in the brief timeline he kept in his notebook and realized that it was hours after the murder of Poker and was even after he had been brought to see Uncle Kage. Did his escape prompt the killer to burn down the warehouse in order to destroy any evidence that might have been inside? If that was the case then it was possible that their criminal lead being connected to the heist held more water than they had originally thought, especially if Poker brought them back to his safehouse to have it double as the planning area for the heist.

As they drove back to the city Alkali took out the files he had found and took a look at them. The killer was probably in these files… and that would make sense for why they attempted to burn down the entire warehouse if he didn't know where they were kept or what Poker had on them. He wished that he had gotten more time to look at those files when they were being shown to him, but other than a brief glance he hadn't seen much that he could go on as far as a name, face, or location of any of the criminals. If only they hadn't been interrupted…

That's right, Alkali said in his own mind, their meeting had been interrupted by someone that was believed to be skulking about the warehouse. At first he had thought that it might have been Xander or Trinity that had done it, but neither of them said they had and he had found them both where he had left them previously before going into the warehouse. Maybe it wasn't the fact that Poker merely was attempting a fake heist, if someone had caught the wolf talking to a private investigator and showing the files he had gathered on them there might be something inside that would drive them to kill. But even as one piece was put into place it just revealed three more pieces he didn't have; what was in the files that someone would kill over and why did the killer only feel threatened when he saw him talking to someone else, or how they even knew what was happening in the first place.

Questions swirled around him like the smoke that had risen up from that warehouse, and just like that burned wreckage it would take some time to reveal the truth like he had done with that grate. Unfortunately as he pulled out his watch and looked at it he saw that it was nearly one in the afternoon, the minutes slipping through his fingers like sand at the beach. When he looked over at Xander he could see the worry on the dragon's face, and what made it worse for Alkali is the guilt that a small voice in the back of his mind wondered if perhaps it hadn't somehow been him. It was only a fleeting thought but his mind made the connection that the dragon knew that he was getting closer to the truth and if there was blackmail info on him that Alkali would find it, but the ferret quickly shook his head of that thought.

No… the true identity of their killer was somewhere in the files that remained clutched to his chest, all he could hope was that they were readable enough for them to find it.

Chapter Six – File Not Found

When Alkali and Xander arrived back at the speakeasy they found all four of the rest of their team hard at work, all of them making sketches on who might have met with Poker in the weeks and months before his death. While Draggor only had one or two that he had seen during his one visit to the place Serathin had been there a few times before to help with Syndicate business and tried to help Trinity and Zen with identifying faces they had sketched. "Looks like the two are back from their fact-finding mission," the imp said as they walked in, the demon sniffing the air as they walked past them. "Man, you smell smokier than me, what happened?"

"Let's just say someone went through a lot of trouble in order to try and destroy these," Alkali replied as he set the dirty files on top of the bar, which earned a glower from the fox while he spread them out. "I know that these aren't ideal but whatever we can find in here to track down those that might have wanted Poker dead is going to be helpful. Now there are four files there so each of you take one to try and glean any information on while I go to the restroom and try to wash up."

The others nodded and they all gathered around to find one to investigate while Alkali and Xander went past the stage and to the washrooms to try and clean the grime from their hands and face. As much as the ferret wished that he could go out and get a fresh change of clothes he had neither the time nor the money in order to do it, and the last thing he needed was to draw attention at a commercial area of the city. Despite Uncle Kage's promise that the information wouldn't be leaked someone had already potentially defied his orders once as he thought back to the conversation that he had with the cockroach. The Kage Syndicate was going to either let Poker go through with the pretend heist or push him into doing it so that they could humiliate him and prevent the FBI from doing further investigations into their activities, which meant that he would have been more protected than most that operated in this city.

It also made Alkali think about Trinity and her role in all of this. Despite revealing that she was actually an ATF agent also trying to bring down the Kage Syndicate she had remained vague on how that was going to happen with her just singing here at the Foxhole each night. Sure it was a place where members of the Syndicate hung out, but why go through all the trouble of monitoring them? Plus they already knew that there was a major bootlegging operation going on in this area, perhaps they were just interested in the flow of alcohol that flooded the streets and tried to find the source.

Alkali quickly shook his head and splashed his face with water in order to clear his thoughts. Why Trinity was here and what she was doing made little difference in the grand scheme of things… unless she was the one that Poker had gotten a file on. An FBI agent finding a dirty ATF agent would have been something to write home about, and it would explain why he shot him in the foot and tried to pursue him after the fact. Once she knew where he was all she had to do was wait for him, and if she was the one skulking around the warehouse while Xander was distracted then she would have known that he was going to meet him at his office.

It was a scenario that Alkali didn't like to think about, but it wasn't be the first time that a dame double-crossed a guy and it wouldn't be the last either. He had to keep his thoughts close to his chest though, if he was right and she sniffed him out then he would be a liability for her just like Poker was. All he could do was run down the leads of the criminals that were in those files and hope that they found something that would point in a different direction… or incriminate her if she was guilty. He just hoped these leads wouldn't end with him getting introduced to a knife as he attempted to wash the last of the ash from his fur before going back out into the main bar.

When he walked back into the speakeasy he saw that Xander was already there and was having a drink while the other four looked over the pages of the files that had been given to him. "Hey Alkali, I don't want to discourage you but I'm not sure how useful you think these pages are going to be," Serathin stated when he looked up and saw the ferret walk in, flipping over the folder to reveal paper that was smeared with blackened soot. "This is worse than when the CIA redacts a sensitive file."

"I might actually have something that might be of some use," Zen chimed in as he walked over towards Alkali to show him his folder. While not as bad as the one that the sabrewolf had there was still a lot of water and fire damage to it, but near the bottom he could see one part that had been spared which had an occupation listed on it. "I recognized this store as a produce supplier that I sometimes use, the booze those bootleggers bring in is so bad sometimes I just mix juices and stuff to try and make it palatable."

"Yes, I've had some of your… what do you call them, cocktails?" Alkali replied. "But that's a major supplier, they must have dozens, if not hundreds of people that work for that chain."

"Ah, but they probably only have one district manager," the fox replied with a grin as he pointed to another line below the employer. "I've heard through the grapevine that this place also smuggles through quite a few illegal narcotics as well as alcohol, so if this Agent Wolf was looking for someone to pretend to get the cash out of the city that operation would be beneficial to him."

"That does make sense," Alkali said as he squinted at the sheet, only to look back up at Zen when he recognized what was said. "Wait, what do you mean we?"

"Well, I have an account there, do you?" Zen asked haughtily, which Alkali shook his head at. "There you go then; I can get you through the first areas of the plant and then you can make your way from there. I can only imagine that this guy is going to be paranoid since someone they were working with to rip off a major criminal organization was murdered, even if it hasn't been on the news yet."

Even though Alkali didn't like the idea of involving someone else in what could potentially be an interrogation he knew the fox was right. The last thing he needed to do was spook whomever he needed to talk to, if they saw him coming and went to ground then he would probably never find them in time. After he agreed he told Zen to come with him to the back alley where he hoped Pandez had remained to give them a lift, and as they walked back the ferret suddenly found another tagging along with them. Trinity had overheard their conversation and had given her folder to Xander so she could come along and also confront this potential smuggler.

Before the detective could even start to try and dissuade her the look that he received from the wolf-dog was enough to convey what she wanted him to know. Even if the murder of Poker and the clearing of Alkali's name took precedence she was still going to look for her own leads in her investigation, whatever that might be. She would also be a valuable asset at this point to expedite the gathering of information if she was willing to break her cover to do so. Part of him wonders if her entire reason for helping him was to try and gather some sort of case before this whole thing is blown open, but once more Trinity continued to keep her cards close to her chest as they walked out into the chill afternoon air.

Though the traffic had started to grow a bit thicker Pandez continued to make good time for them to get through the city. The produce provider they were looking for was called Leafy Greens and it was one of the largest providers of fruits and vegetables for the city. The bootlegger panda dropped them off at the front door and informed them he would be in a parking garage about a block away if they needed him before he drove down the street after they got out. Though Alkali looked around and noticed that they were a bit out of place among those wearing overalls and leather gloves Zen immediately walked inside like he owned the place.

Alkali and Trinity both decided to follow the fox's lead on this one and watched as he went over to someone he clearly knew, and after a few minutes of conversing with the jaguar Zen came back to the two of them with an excited look in his eyes. "Alright, so the one we're looking for is Miles Anderson," Zen explained. "He has an office on the other side of the building and from what my friend told me he has been in there all morning."

"Seems like we finally have a bit of luck on our side," Trinity stated as she looked over where Zen had said the offices were, which were quite some distance away. "Did you find anything else about him?"

"Not much else," Zen replied as they began to walk over. "He did say he's quite the bull."

"So he's short-tempered…" Alkali stated, only for the fox to give him a look before shaking his head slightly.

"No… he's an actual bull," Zen corrected. "But from the way he spoke about him perhaps this guy does have a short fuse. Do you want me to go first and try to see if he's in?"

"I think it'll look strange at this point if we split up at all," Alkali said. "Let's just stay together and hope that your bravado is enough to get us to where we need to go."

As the three continued to make their way past a number of conveyors that held all manner of produce he could see that more than a few pairs of eyes watched them as they walked past. If they hadn't been spotted coming in news of their arrival was definitely known now, and for Alkali he wondered if that was a good or bad thing. Anyone running a smuggling operation through this place would probably think that the three of them, or at least one of them was a cop that was trying to bust them, and his suspicions were becoming more confirmed as he saw the glances they were getting were increasingly nervous in nature. So far no one had attempted to approach them though and it seemed to the ferret that both sides were being very cautious of one another.

Despite this Zen continued to lead the way towards the back office area while giving the occasional nod to those that he passed by. His very presence seemed to put the workers more at ease, as if they could sense the criminal in their midst and were comforted by it. It turned out to be a boon for him to come along after all, Alkali thought to himself as they finally got to the wrought-iron stairwell that led to the second floor. The offices themselves were open to the rest of the sorting facility and connected by a balcony, and just as they were about to step foot on it they saw a rather large bull man step out of one of the doors and looked out at the production plant.

"Hey you!" Zen said suddenly, which prompted both Alkali and Trinity as well as the bull to look at him. "Stay right there, we have some questions for you!"

That was definitely not the right thing to say, Alkali thought to himself as he saw a look of fear suddenly come over him. Before any of them could react the muscular male leapt over the railing and down onto one of the conveyor belts, his hooves squashing the pumpkins that were riding up before sprinting down back down into the factory itself. With his only lead racing away from them the ferret the detective found himself kicking into action, moving back down the stairs as fast as he could in order to match pace with the fleeing suspect. The other workers quickly moved aside as he pulled out his gun and shouted at Miles to freeze, only for his order to fall on deaf ears.

When Alkali saw that the bull had a straight shot to the loading bays on the conveyor belt he rode he knew that he had to do something to stop him or lose him forever, and as he got close enough to one of the sorting bays he used the bin to hop up to one of the belts himself. For a few moments he teetered back and forth a few times as he got used to the movement of the machine beneath him before he ran forward once more. More than once he nearly tripped over the radishes that he had to hop over, but fortunately his belt not only ran in the same direction as the one the bull was on but also ran a bit faster. Despite the other man clomping down the conveyor at full speed Alkali managed to catch up with him and with a daring leap tackled him off into one of the large bins below.

The two landed with a dull thud into the leafy vegetable bins and despite having the wind knocked out of him Alkali found himself fighting with the bull that attempted to get away. The two wrestled back and forth and though the other man was stronger than him Alkali knew enough dirty tricks to keep his head above the vegetables they were fighting in. Eventually the bull had managed to pin him down against the deep green leaves, but as the ferret struggled against his grip he managed to grab a handful of them and shove them into the mouth of the bull. As he gagged and sputtered Alkali managed to push himself down to get out of the grasp of the other man and get up, drawing the gun he had managed to grab once more and pointing it at the bovine while also spitting out a bit of the vegetable that had gotten his mouth.

"Ugh, so bitter, what is this stuff…" Alkali said as he watched the bull continue to try and get the fistful of ruffage out, the ferret looking over at the sign on the bin they were in. "Kale? Kale?!"

"What's wrong?" Trinity shouted as she and Zen got up to him, looking at him in confusion as he realized he was shouting.

"I just… I don't want to talk about it," Alkali replied before once more focusing on the bull that had just managed to recover himself. "Alright Miles, spill it, what information do you have on the wolf with the red eye marking that you met with?"

"What?" The bull asked in confusion, still coughing up a bit of the kale as he looked at Alkali. "What the hell are you talking about?"

The detective tilted his head in confusion and looked over at Zen, who just shrugged his shoulders, before going back to the bull. "Are you not Miles Anderson the district manager?" Alkali asked, his gun slowly lowering when the bovine shook his head with a genuinely confused look on his face. "Well who are you then?"

"I'm Steve, I run the logistics desk for the shipping department," the bull said. "Why did you think I was Miles?"

"Because you ran!" Trinity exclaimed in exasperation as Steve pulled out his identification that had his name and occupation on it. "Why did you do that if you weren't the one we were looking for?"

"I… don't know…" Steve replied with a shrug of his shoulders before he leaned in to Alkali. "Look, I may have a warrant or three for supplying bootleggers with their hops and barley, but that was at another job with another name. When you three came rolling up on the office like that and then shouted at me I thought you were going to bust me for sure."

"Great… just perfect," Trinity said as Alkali slowly got out of the kale bin, trying to shake out what remained of the produce in his clothes like trying to get a spider off of himself. "Well I think Miles knows why we're coming now, it'll be a miracle if he didn't run."

Though Alkali didn't want to feel that pessimistic he knew that the wolfdog spoke the truth. Not only had they chased the wrong guy through a produce plant and destroyed several bins of now worthless vegetables they basically announced their attentions to try and interrogate a bull man. After apologizing to Steve for chasing him down the three made their way back towards the offices, this time with all eyes on them. Alkali realized that there was a secondary problem to their impromptu chase in that someone was likely to have called the police on their antics, and he doubted that even the Kage Syndicate could hide his being a suspect to murder if he got caught.

At this point however the only thing Alkali found himself focusing on was talking to Miles and hopefully getting a lead on whomever killed Poker. Perhaps he was the one who did it, but the ferret knew that was putting the cart before the horse as they got to the back of the building once more. Zen made sure to keep an eye out in case anyone else tried to run while Akali and Trinity made their way up to the second-floor offices. Once they were on the balcony they passed by the office that Steve had come out of and saw that it was in fact the office for the shipping coordinator. The ferret tried not to shake his head and told himself to calm down to not make any more mistakes as he and Trinity found the door that belonged to the district manager.

They gave a knock on the door and Trinity asked if Miles was in, to which they got no response. With the frosted glass that made up the windows it was impossible to tell if he was inside or not as Alkali trained an ear to make sure he didn't try to escape through some sort of back exit. The office was completely silent however and he began to wonder if what Zen's friend told him about the bull being in his office was false. After another set of tries to bring Miles to the door failed both gave one another a small nod and Alkali slowly opened the door while Trinity stayed back while brandishing her pistol. The door swung inward slightly and when nothing moved to attack them the ferret poked his head in to see if he could see the bull inside, only to swear under his breath and rush in with Trinity right behind him.

Inside the office Alkali rushed forward to the bull that was sitting at his chair with a plastic bag tied over his head, but even before he got close he knew that Miles Anderson had been dead for at least a few hours before they had gotten there. Both of them looked on in shock at what they saw and when Zen came in to join them he let out a slight gasp of surprise as well. Miles Anderson killed himself at his desk in his office… or at least that's what someone wanted those who found the body to think. Part of him couldn't believe that his only insight into who might have framed him had decided to punch his own ticket instead of getting caught, but as they looked around they didn't see any sign of a struggle and as Trinity walked over to the other side of the desk she pointed out a piece of paper that had something written on it.

"To whom it may concern," Alkali read out loud as Zen began to look underneath the body while Trinity checked out the other papers on his desk. "I have realized just now that I have done something terrible, and even though it didn't happen my mere involvement in it is enough to condemn me to death anyway. I only hope this act shows my remorse and this note shows that I didn't mean to target who we did, please show mercy on my family."

"A suicide note," Trinity exclaimed once Alkali had finished. "Hell of way to go, suffocating yourself like that. What could possibly make him so scared that he would do this instead of trying to run or something like that?"

"That's one of many questions," Alkali replied as he rubbed his head, then turned to see that their breach into his office had not gone unnoticed. A young rabbit woman stood there at the threshold with wide eyes that were fixated right on the dead bull man and the ones that were around him, which caused the ferret to realize what it looked like and quickly rose his hands up. "Wait, hold on, just… let us explain…"

The woman would not wait however and soon the air was filled with her shrieks for someone to call the police. "So now we have to run," Zen said as he got up from his hands and knees and put a coffee cup on the desk. "Nothing underneath him but an empty mug, looks like he didn't take the time to finish his morning beverage before wrapping things up so to speak."

"Nothing in his desk either," Trinity added in as she shut the last drawer in frustration. "If he was smuggling he either cleaned his tracks before he killed himself or was really good at not leaving a trail. I think we need to just accept that this is a literal dead end and hope that the next three potential leads pan out."

Alkali didn't like the sound of that but there was nothing he could do, especially when he kept looking at the bug-eyed expression of the deceased bovine beneath the layer of plastic that had ended his life. With only a few minutes until the police came and nothing around the body there wasn't much that indicated anything but a suicide, but even that in itself was strange. It sounded like he had just found out that the people they were planning to rob was the Kage Syndicate, and if that was true and he didn't know it was fake he could have been scared enough to go through with the act to avoid being captured. It was just something about the way the suicide note was written bothered him… but he didn't have much time to think about it as he saw others starting to gather around the doorframe while gasping in shock and awe.

This definitely wasn't going to help his case, Alkali thought to himself as he told the other two to clear out. Just as he was about to do the same he took one last look around the room in order to try and give himself an accurate mental picture in case it was needed. Bull dead at his desk with plastic bag duct taped around his head, suicide note in front of him, pile of papers on the side of his desk, coffee mug, motivational poster on opposite wall, a bunch of plants and flowers growing along another wall, frosted window glass, and a half-full trash can. Once he believed he had committed everything to memory he ran out with the rest of them, heading to the back door as he heard others starting to shout from the office area as well.

The three managed to get out of the building without a lot of interference, but as they went around to the main street they could start to hear sirens coming up in the distance. While it wasn't the same precinct that had arrested Alkali for murder it wouldn't matter if he was put back into the system again, and everyone had saw them leave so they knew where they had gone if the police asked them. As they looked around for a way to escape Zen pointed to a spot they could go unnoticed, though both Trinity and Alkali looked at it in distain. It was a small river that ran through this section of the city, the water murky enough that even someone just a few inches beneath the surface couldn't be seen. The three looked at each other, then with time running out they jumped in to the freezing cold water as the cop cars zoomed overhead just a few seconds later.

Almost immediately Alkali could feel his muscles start to seize as he remained in the icy embrace of the river, only able to stand it for about a minute before he had to either get out or risk floating down the entirety of it as a corpse. The others weren't far behind and fortunately they had managed to get far enough where their path ran through a small grove of trees behind a few small commercial buildings. "I think I change my mind," Trinity said through chattering teeth as the frigid air seemed to seep into their soaked bodies until it reached their bones. "I don't want to do this anymore."

"Hey, we're all implicated in that man's death now," Zen said as he squeezed out the water from his jacket while seemingly impervious to the cold himself. "I'm sure they have sketches of all three of us by now so they can question us about why we were there when he died."

"But clearly he died by suicide," Trinity stated as they climbed up the embankment and around the back lots until they reached a restaurant exhausted vent they could stand under to warm up. "Why would they look for us?"

"They probably will call it a suicide," Alkali said suddenly as he shook his head, though part of it was from the intense shivering that still went through his body. "But I don't think it was, too many things don't add up."

"Oh?" Zen said simply.

"Let's not discuss it here," Alkali stated as he looked out from behind the restaurant to see if there were any cops around before shaking his coat to try and get the excess water, which started to crystallize into ice, from it. "Pandez should be somewhat close by, let's get back to Zen's bar and I'll fill everyone in on what I saw. We need to start being extremely careful, whoever killed Poker is deciding not to leave any loose ends."

Trinity and Zen glanced at one another before looking back at Alkali, but the detective was already working on the way to get to the parking lot where their ride was. Even with the heat from the exhaust vent keeping them warm they couldn't stay underneath it forever, especially since they were still shivering. They also couldn't risk going inside either in case someone wondered what three very wet people were doing just walking into a diner or clothing store. It was then that the ferret saw the large boxes that had probably come from the delivery to the restaurant and got an idea…

Meanwhile in the parking lot about a block away from the produce center Pandez listened to the radio while waiting for Alkali and the others to return, only to immediately slouch in his seat when he saw the sirens of the police cars streak by. He remained bent over in his cab for a few minutes until he was sure that he didn't hear anything else, then got up and started his engine in order to leave. "Sorry guys," he said as he gave one last look to make sure there weren't any cops around him. "Looks like you're finding your own way home."

Just as he was about to back out however he felt a loud bang on his driver side door and looked down to see someone with multiple layers of cardboard wrapped around his body. "Listen, I don't have any change," Pandez said as he rolled down the window slightly. "Please stand back so I can leave."

"It's us Pandez!" Alkali whispered loudly, looking up from the layers he had wrapped himself in to keep as much heat as possible. "The other two are climbing in the back now, let me in the passenger side!"

Though the bootlegger looked at him apprehensively he sighed and unlocked the other door, allowing Alkali to scramble inside after ditching the cardboard cocoon he had made. He still found himself shivering and put his hands against the heater in the car as Pandez looked at him incredulously. "It's a long story," the ferret exclaimed. "Just get us out of here and back to the Foxhole."

The panda knew enough to not ask questions and instead get back on the road, only stopping momentarily when he saw two more pairs of hands attempt to reach through the window between the cab and the back in order to try and get at the heat coming from the front. As they raced away from the growing police presence and back to their section of the city Alkali couldn't help but frown as he thought of his deteriorating situation. When he opened his pocket watch he had to wipe off the condensation to see that this had taken up most of his afternoon and they were about to track into the evening. That meant that they wouldn't be able to use the speakeasy as their base of operations since Zen needed to open it to keep up appearances, and Xander wouldn't be able to bring them all to his apartment without raising suspicion.

For the detective however the more pressing matter was that they had gotten cut off from the one person that could possibly tell them what was going on with Poker that might have gotten him killed. Even though he couldn't speak to him the fact that Miles had either committed suicide or had gotten murdered himself did give him a few clues that he didn't have before. It was clear that the death of the FBI agent was not some random act of violence, and he guessed that the other three names on those files would also either be dead or have gone to ground. It also seemed that Uncle Kage might have not been exactly so cavalier when it came to someone planning a heist against his gala event, but he couldn't go after that lead unless he had concrete proof that the cockroach was somehow behind it.

When he filled in the other two on what his thoughts were they both nodded and added a few of their own ideas in the mix. Despite all their conjecture though the one thing that they couldn't figure out by the time they got back to the speakeasy was who killed Miles, and that was the one question that Alkali needed answered by the time his forty-eight hours were up. The only thing they could hope for was that when they got back the others had figured out who the remaining three members in Poker's makeshift crew were and if any of them were still alive. At this point it was a race with the killer to see who got to them first, and Alkali found himself gritting his teeth when he had to admit the killer was winning…

Chapter Seven – Trapped like a Rat

Once they had gotten inside the speakeasy Zen went to his kitchen to warm up some tea while Trinity and Alkali were wrapped in blankets that the fox had stored away for emergencies. As they tried to warm up their bodies while in their wet outfits they were given more bad news by Xander; they had managed to decipher another file and figured out that it was a security specialist named Patrick, but when they called the apartment complex that was listed they found out the panther had taken a bath with his toaster sometime that morning. That meant there were only two suspects left on the list, with one of them being so damaged that they could hardly make out any words much less information that would help lead to finding him. The other file did have some usable information, but as day turned to night the only thing they could find out was that it was a python man who specialized in safe cracking.

"Listen, I don't want to have to put you guys out but I can't be having FBI files scattered about my illegal booze den," Zen said as he began to put unmarked bottles underneath the bar. "Also if we're going to keep going about as normal then Trinity is slated to sing for tonight and I don't have any back-ups."

"It's fine," Trinity said with a small nod. "I think my time as a detective might be coming to an end after taking that dip in the South River. If you find anything else though do keep me informed, I would love to find out what happens."

Alkali tried to not let his feelings show as the wolfdog sauntered towards the stage, knowing that she was tougher than that but was trying not to blow her cover. He had to admit that she was pretty good at the game, which made him wonder if he could believe anything that she had said to him. Once again the thought of her being the killer crossed his mind; with both men on the team having died sometime during the early morning it was possible that her, or anyone in the group or that she had met, had torched the warehouse and killed them before he had even gotten up that morning. Whoever had met Poker and the others already knew their identities and didn't need the files, which also meant they could also the remaining survivor could identify the one that was killing them off.

The group decided it would be best for Alkali to go with Xander back to his apartment while Draggor and Serathin tried to run down some leads on the safe cracker that was either dead or in hiding, and though the ferret wanted to protest he heard a loud growl in his stomach that reminded him he hadn't eaten anything since breakfast. He was also still potentially suffering from hypothermia and had been running around the city all day attempting to clear his name. He still had over a day to go before Uncle Kage would throw him to the wolves and he would do no one any good if he collapsed from sheer exhaustion. After Xander gave the others their number they took a cab back to his place; while Pandez had been more than eager to continue with their search it came time for him to make deliveries of the bathtub booze and he had to go make sure it arrived to the speakeasies of the city that opened for business.

As they drove back to the reporter's apartment Alkali didn't say a word, his mind deciphering the clues that he had collected so far in order to try and find the one that framed him. The major problem was that the killer had been cleaning up his tracks before he had even started the case; the fact that two criminals that had joined Poker's crew both committed suicide on the same morning and wrote similar letters begging for the forgiveness of the Kage Syndicate was just too neat and tidy. Part of him wished he could go and investigate the crime scene of the security expert's apartment, but he felt like they were pushing their luck just by riding in a cab. The ferret felt his brain pulsing in the skull with all the information he was attempting to process as the one murder that he had been focusing on suddenly turned to three with two more potentially out there.

Alkali was in such a daze that he hardly realized that they had gotten to Xander's apartment until he suddenly found himself on his couch in front of the small fake fireplace he had, though when he had gathered where he was he saw that the dragon was nowhere to be found. As he shifted about he found himself sitting on a towel and figured that he was getting a fresh set of clothes for him, the ferret grateful he had the foresight to leave a few sets here when he stayed the night. By this point the warmth was starting to banish the cold that had continued to pervade through his muscles and he started to feel his eyelids droop with only the gnawing hunger in his stomach keeping him awake. For a second he felt himself dip forward before his head shot back up and his eyes opened wide.

"Yeah, seems like you've been through a lot," a voice said that caused Alkali to turn, the ferret blinking several times as he saw the familiar visage of the black-furred wolf look back at him. As he sat there on the couch he could still see the slit in his neck where his throat had been cut, something that was widened every time the lupine spoke. "I think we've both had a hard couple of days."

"I… would say so…" Alkali replied as he slowly turned around to see if Xander was there, then turned his head to see that Poker was still there next to him. "You look good though, for being dead…"

"Actually I'm just your brain attempting to figure out this case by manifesting the victim thanks to your near-hypothermic state combined with hunger and fatigue," Poker explained. "But if it helps catch my killer I'm happy to help however I can."

Even though Alkali knew that he was either dreaming or hallucinating it was the first time that he had seen a victim brought back to life in his mind. Of course, most of his cases didn't involve dead bodies, in fact he tried to stay away from those as much as possible. But if his brain was doing this it meant at the very least he might be on the right train of thought or that his mind had made a connection in his sub-conscious that he hadn't made yet. Either way it was extremely disturbing to see the dead wolf sitting nonchalantly next to him with those blue eyes that he had had last seen glassed over with the glaze of death.

"I don't suppose you can tell me who killed you," Alkali stated, which prompted the wolf to chuckle before he held his neck in pain.

"Trust me, if I could I would," Poker replied. "This killer has you chasing your own tail though, you're trying to see the big picture when all the information you need is narrower in focus. You know that something is wrong with the scene of your office where the murder took place, you need to go back and figure out what it is."

Alkali sighed and closed his eyes, and when he opened them again he was shocked to find himself standing in his office with Poker standing in about the same spot where he had found his body. Everything looked exactly the way he had left it before going out to crash the interview at the Foxhole, and as he looked over the scene again he suddenly saw a shadowy figure appear in the room as well. He guessed it was the manifestation of the murderer and as he watched the ghostly image went over and grabbed Poker from behind. It was the way he assumed the murderer would have done it, either bash him on the head or cut his throat and the resulting fall caused the damage.

As he watched it unfold in his mind Alkali felt a spark in the back of his mind, the recognition that something about the way the fight played out and how the scene ended up didn't make any sense. He watched it again and tried a slightly different scenario but once again there was nothing he could see that would help him figure out what his brain was trying to show him. Was it the fact that he didn't find anything that had blood on it from the head wound? No, the killer could have easily wiped off anything he used or it might not have caused enough initial damage for a blood transfer.

But that line of thinking began to feel like he was on track to something, and though he hated watching the agent get murdered over and over again he needed to figure out how the killer did it to add a piece to the puzzle. As Alkali moved over to get a different angle he suddenly heard a voice that he hadn't before, his ears perking up as he wondered if he was getting another clue. Slowly the sound grew louder until he recognized the voice as... Xander?

"Hey, wake up!" Xander practically shouted as Alkali suddenly felt himself being shaken. The ferret let out a gasp as he suddenly opened his eyes and looked around to see the blue-scaled dragon in a Hawaiian bathrobe practically sitting on top of him while on the couch. "I made dinner and got you clothes, I figure after the day you've had it was the least I could do."

Though he couldn't be mad at Xander for waking him Alkali thought that he might have been on some sort of breakthrough with the case, but when he looked over to his side he saw that Poker was gone and the moment had past. As he was helped to his feet he took a glance at his pocket watch and saw that he was getting close to his first twenty-four hours being gone, which means he had only one day left until he was served up to the FBI like a sacrificial lamb. At the moment though the only thing he could think about was the hot shower he was helped into and the warm clothes he had been given, followed quickly by the hot meal that Xander had prepared for him. For the briefest of moments it was as if all the bad things that had happened to him up to this point was just a nightmare, but his mind was quick to remind him that there were still sharks circling the waters waiting for his raft to sink.

At some point after dinner he had managed to pull himself to bed and get to sleep, and though he had hoped that he would find himself back in the dream version of his office the only thing that greeted him on the other side was pure darkness. When he awoke again he was surprised to find that his eyes opened and he was still shrouded in shadow, though as his eyes adjusted to the light he could see the faint lights of the city beyond in the window of the dragon's bedroom. As he began to sit upright he could feel his body protest with pain and he found himself flopping back down before he could catch himself. As he laid there staring at the ceiling he heard what had caused him to awaken in the first place, hearing Xander in the next room saying something on the telephone.

Eventually the strength returned to Alkali's limbs and he got up once more, though he still felt worse than having a pre-prohibition hangover as he went to the living room just as the dragon hung up. "Your ears must have been burning," Xander said as they changed back into their street clothes. "That was Draggor down at the Foxhole, they said that they might have a lead on the safe cracker's whereabouts. You think you're up for a little midnight gallivanting around town?"

"You could put a saddle on my back and ride me down main street if it meant catching the killer," Alkali replied as he grabbed the coat that hung from the wall and put it around him, the material already dry as he made sure his watch was in his breast pocket and his gun was on his hip. "Let's just try and get there before the killer does."

Another cab ride later and Alkali once more found himself in front of the Foxhole, the moose at the door letting both him and Xander in without any fuss. It appeared Zen had already knew of their arrival and had cleared the path for them to get to the bar without trouble. The inside of the speakeasy was packed and as it was already a bit late people had clearly had their fill of the bootleg gin warming their own bellies. On stage Trinity was continuing to sing to the masses in order to keep them entertained, though for the ferret the only thing he had eyes for was the imp that sat in one corner with the draconic sabrewolf next to him.

Though he tried to remain nonchalant Alkali couldn't help but push several people aside in order to get to the two criminals as quickly as possible. "So you found him?" Alkali asked excitedly. "The safecracker is here?"

"No, but we have a lead on someone that would know where they're hiding," Draggor said in a hushed tone just above the jazz music being played. "Serathin saw The Rat come in."

"Oh, let me guess," Alkali said as he put his hands in the air. "He's a rat guy, right?"

Serathin and Draggor looked at one another before turning and shaking their heads in unison. "Nah, this guy just happens to know every good hiding spot in the city," Serathin explained as Alkali dragged his hands down his face in exasperation. "Since no one fitting the description of the safecracker has turned up dead he probably found out the other two or three are dead with Poker and decided to lay low. If we can get The Rat to spill the beans on someone that recently requested his services then we might find him before the killer does."

Alkali nodded and allowed the two to go and confront the one they were talking about while he sat at the table they had occupied. With the potential new lead coming the ferret suddenly felt full of energy to the point where he found himself fidgeting while he waited. While Xander attempted to keep him calmed down he knew that he couldn't, especially when he saw the imp and hybrid come back with an otter in tow behind them. It was clear that the one known as The Rat was also nervous about talking, but after repeated assurances that no one would know that he squealed and this was to clear Alkali's name the otter sat up on the stool that Xander had just slid off of.

"So, I'm sure that my two friends here filled you in on the problem we're currently having," Alkali said, the otter nodding slightly. "Now normally I would a hundred precent respect the privacy that you're trying to give your clients, but this happens to be a matter of life and death and if we don't catch a killer in twenty-four hours he's going to be free to do it again. Now three people have already been murdered, if you tell us where the python safecracker is hiding then we can keep it from being four."

"Look, it's not like I don't want to help out the city's most famous detective and have him owe me a favor," The Rat said as he looked around. "But with cops clamping down on illegal activity across the board and crime organizations starting to actually feel the pinch criminals for hire are starting to be short supply and that starts to cut into my business. If I give up my contact and he ends up getting arrested or getting killed than no one will ever come to me again."

"I already said that we're trying to help this person," Draggor chimed in.

"If your guy is still alive then he probably knows someone is after him," Alkali explained. "If he can tell us who it is than the Kage Syndicate will step in and make sure they are brought to justice and everyone can continue doing business as usual. Otherwise the feds might step in if they don't think that one of their own was killed by a private investigator, and if you think the pinch is bad right now just wait until the feds give crime in this city a squeeze."

The otter swallowed hard at that and nodded, Alkali feeling his hopes rise slightly as The Rat took a piece of paper out of his jacket and wrote something on it. "This is one of the best safe houses that I have in the city," The Rat explained as he scribbled an address on it before sliding it to the ferret. "All the doors and windows are wired to shutter close if the panic button is pushed, and if that happens the only one that can open it is myself. When you knock on the door he's going to ask you if it's the pizza delivery guy, and all you have to do is respond that you have a large cheese with pineapple and anchovy for him."

Alkali nodded and thanked The Rat for his cooperation, the otter quickly leaving the detective and going back into the crowd. The ferret looked at his pocket watch and saw that it was nearly two am, which meant that if he wasn't sleeping he would likely be a suspicious guest to start. But on the other paw if the killer somehow finds out this information than he would have far greater problems than a couple of late-night guests at his door. When he relayed the plan to the other two they agreed to go with him, and though Xander also volunteered Alkali told him to go back to the apartment and wait for them there.

Though the dragon didn't appear to be happy with being left behind Alkali knew that him just being in the neighborhood in question was going to throw up alarm bells, much less a reporter being there as well. He also could take the call if Zen and Trinity found any more people that might help them figure out who the last file is on since they had very little else that was gleaned on the black-smeared pages. With Draggor and Serathin the three went out to the alley, this time taking the imp's car in order to make their way to the area marked out for them by The Rat. As they passed by the stage Alkali looked up at the wolfdog and he saw her give him a small nod, the ferret responding by tipping his hat before taking the back exit out.

When they got to the imp's car however they suddenly heard a string of cursing come from Draggor as he suddenly rushed forward and knelt down by the front tire of his car. "You've got to be kidding me," Draggor said as both Alkali and Serathin saw that the tire was completely flat. "This winter weather, it's the second flat I've gotten this season. I already used my spare too."

"Well that's rough," Serathin stated as he held his arms, his breath forming clouds between his saberteeth as Draggor continued to inspect it. "So now what do we do, wait for the bus? Hail a cab?"

"Last thing I want anyone to be able to do is track us to the next potential scene of a murder," Alkali said as he paced back and forth slightly. "It's late enough in the night, maybe that bootlegger is done with his deliveries and can give us a lift. Zen has the number of a few other gin joints where he could try get a hold of the panda if he's not at his base of operations, if not then we're going to have to find some other means of transportation."

Alkali left the demon and sabrewolf to continue to lament over the flat tire as he went back into the Foxhole. By this point the party had started to wind down and people were leaving quickly, not wanting to be caught by the roving bands of cops that were looking for drunks that they could trace back to their watering holes. Zen was cleaning the glasses that were left in the bar and when he went up to it, stopping when he saw the ferret approach.

"Hey, could you contact that Pandez guy that delivers for you?" Alkali asked.

"I can try," Zen replied. "Why, I thought Draggor had managed to get a vehicle for you guys."

"Flat tire," Alkali explained simply. "It might be a coincidence, but I don't like the fact that the second we get a lead on where this python is staying my friend suddenly springs a flat. If you can't get a hold of him then perhaps could you or Trinity lend us something?"

"I don't think that Trinity even has a car, and even if she did I let her leave as soon as I started shutting down the bar," Zen explained. "As for me I don't really do a lot of driving, if I have to go anywhere I just grab a cab or take the bus like everyone else. I'll call a few other speakeasies and if Pandez is at one of them I'll see if I can't get him to pick you guys up, otherwise you might just have to wait until morning to head over there."

Wait until morning… that was something that Alkali didn't want to hear as he watched the fox go back towards the area where his phone was and start to make calls to summon the bootlegger. Not only did that cut in to what precious little time he had left but every second he had the knowledge of where the python was staying but unable to act on it felt like the killer was edging out in front of him. It was like this person could see into his mind and knew exactly what he was going to do, except that he kept beating him to the punch. Between the fires and the deaths of the other two members of the crew the ferret could feel the noose slowly start to tighten around his own neck to the point he started to find it hard to breathe.

Alkali found himself reaching over the bar and grabbing one of the mostly empty bottles, not caring what was inside as he took a drink straight from it. Almost immediately he knew the mistake he had made as the straight homemade liquor burned all the way down to his stomach, causing him to nearly double over and drop the bottle. This damn prohibition, Alkali thought to himself as he continued to clutch his stomach with one hand while putting the bottle back with the other. If he had just had his own supply he could be at his office with a pleasant buzz while watching the world outside, not stuck in a speakeasy hoping some bootlegger would give him a ride so they could clear his name of murder.

After a few minutes the burning sensation passed and Alkali relaxed back onto the stool, the heat of the room subsiding as his body slowly absorbed the mistake he had made. He realized that he had started to lose control of himself in his desperation, something that the killer likely wanted. Once the clock ran out it would be the ferret that got sent off for the crime he didn't commit while the killer went free. Alkali had to solve the murder before time ran out, all his opponent had to do was run out the clock and they would just call it a simple murder of passion or something of that nature.

While Alkali put his head in his hands he suddenly heard the voice of Zen speak up once more. "Looks like you're in luck," the fox said as he came back over towards him. "Pandez had just finished his last run right as I called a nearby gin joint and he said that he was willing to come over and pick you guys up, said he would be here in about fifteen minutes."

"That's… that's great," Alkali replied as he put his fingers against his forehead, still feeling a bit of the fire from the alcohol deep in his throat. "I wish The Rat had given us a phone number for his safe house, we could call and make sure that he hasn't died a horrific death yet before we got there."

Zen frowned at the statement, the fox sighing as he went back to cleaning the cups that were in front of him. "Look, no one is going to say that you've had it easy these past few days," Zen exclaimed. "But you keep talking like that and everyone is going to start to think you gave up. Now I don't know you as well as the others around here, but if the mere stories I've heard of your exploits are even half true than I know you are not someone that throws in the towel right when things get hard."

"I'm still just wondering how I managed to get to this place at all," Alkali finally replied as Zen poured him a glass of a clear liquid, the ferret making a face as he took a sip and realized it was just water. "A few days ago I was just minding my own business when someone came in and asked me to look into a big robbery they overheard; now I have dead FBI agents and criminals and warehouse fires and a potential life sentence hanging over my head, which if I don't solve this case in twenty-one hours I'll be handed over to police by the most powerful criminal organization in the city. I know I shouldn't tempt fate by saying it, but I'm not really sure how things could get much worse for me at this point."

"Well, when you're at the bottom there's nowhere else to go but up," Zen replied as he motioned for Alkali to continue to drink down the glass. "You assembled yourself a good team here to help you out, if anyone is going to help you beat this guy it's going to be all of us together. Plus I wouldn't want to lose one of my best customers just because they got caught in some small murder charge."

Alkali found himself chuckling despite himself and thanked Zen for the water, though when he saw the fox curl his fingers the ferret rolled his eyes and put a nickel in the palm of his hand before leaving. When he looked at his watch he saw that that it was getting close to when Pandez would pick them up and got off of the barstool. Even though his investigation had been going poorly up to that point he always knew that some setbacks were inevitable in the process. The fact they were all happening so quickly meant that potentially he had gotten them out of the way and he was on the way to finding the true culprit. As he passed by the empty stage and headed back towards the alley where the rum runner truck was waiting for him already he couldn't help but give one last look at it before continuing on outside into the dead night beyond.

Chapter Eight – Finding an Eyewitness

As the truck sped down the empty streets of the city Alkali couldn't help but continue to rub the piece of paper in his hand. With their course already plotted there was no more need for it, yet the detective couldn't help but keep it in his hands. It was as if the killer might somehow get a hold of it even if he tore it up and threw it out the window, though his bigger fear was getting there and finding that they had been dead for a long time. From what The Rat had told Draggor and Serathin though he had been approached in the early morning for a safe house and he had been transferred there in the afternoon, likely just about the same time they had discovered the demise of Miles at his desk. If the killer had intended on wiping out the entire crew that morning it was possible that a fluke change in schedule kept this python from having a similar staged suicide.

While the lights of the street whizzed by outside of the car window Alkali could see that it had started to snow again, and it reminded him of when he had opened his window in order to escape after discovering the body in his office. Once again his mind seemed to try and bring him back to that one moment in time, but there were no clues there that could help him with who had actually broken in and murdered Poker. "Something on your mind Alkali?" the voice of the demon brought Alkali back to reality once more. "Hope you're not stressing out too much about the time left on the clock."

Something else he wished he hadn't been reminded of, Alkali thought to himself as he took the pocket watch out and looked at it to see the hour hand move inexhaustibly towards its final destination. "I'm just hoping this guy knows something that makes all of this worth it," the ferret responded. "If we go there and he turns out to have gotten spooked because of some bookie debt he owes or the husband of the wife he was sleeping with behind his back I will not be a happy ferret."

"I'm sure it'll be fine," Serathin replied from the back seat with a grin on his face. "We'll go there, clear Alkali's name, and be back for drinks before the sun goes back down again. Of course, they'll probably still keep your office under lockdown pending a full investigation, and by then I'm sure the dried blood is going to be a nightmare to get out of your floorboards if it soaked in."

Alkali just nodded at that, though in reality he didn't care what happened to his office after this entire ordeal. He just wanted it all to be over, to have the Kage Syndicate off his back and to no longer be wanted by the police as well as restore his standing as a private investigator. There was no doubt though that the cockroach would probably expect some sort of favor from him in exchange for keeping the cops off of his back, not to mention the one that he owed The Rat for the address he had gotten. His marker was starting to get spread all over town, though if he went to jail for murdering an FBI agent they would be good for no one in this city.

When they finally got to the address it was nearly three in the morning as they pulled up to the large apartment building. It was not the best part of town and even with the extremely cold temperatures outside they could still see a few people standing outside. No one would probably think of trying to find their target in his neighborhood at least, Alkali thought to himself as the three got out of the car. Thankfully their presence seemed to have gone unnoticed as they began to walk up to the rather large sprawl, and looked up at the windows that were all lined with various fire escapes. With the number that they were given for the apartment they counted up and over until they believed they were looking at the one that belonged to the safe cracking python.

"Why don't I shimmy up the fire escape and see if anyone is home," Serathin said as they walked over towards the ladder that connected to the one beneath the safe house window. "No point in alerting anyone to our presence inside if we don't have to."

"I mean, you can if you want," Alkali said as he saw the ice-covered metal dangling above them. "I can tell you from experience that those things are a nightmare to get down." The draconic sabrewolf just smirked and took a few steps back, then ran forward and leapt up against the wall itself before bouncing off of it and upwards onto the fire escape. The ferret and imp watched with amazement as the hybrid grabbed onto the bottom rung of the suspended ladder and flipped himself up to land on the other side of the railing.

"Show off," Draggor grumbled as he covered his head to avoid the small shards of ice that came down.

"Come on, it's the first thing you learn in cat burglar school," Serathin replied with a smirk as he stuck out his tongue at them. "Now you two just wait your pretty little heads down there while I go and make sure that our guy is in."

The two watched him quickly scale up the stairs until they had to practically crane their heads to see, once more shielding their faces from snow that got knocked off as he went up the eight floors to the apartment they were looking for. Alkali felt his stomach tie in knots that wasn't related to his hunger as he waited for the sabrewolf to look inside and hopefully find their python still inside and breathing. In only took a few minutes before the thief got up and slowly peaked inside the dark window, then seemed to do a double take and bob his head up completely. Even though they were very far away the look of concern on the face of the hybrid caused the ferret's heart to drop into his feet.

"The shudders are closed!" Serathin shouted. "The window is completely blocked off!"

The announcement made Alkali's blood freeze in his veins. If the shudders were closed that meant that something had happened to their last remaining lead, and if the killer had gotten to him than it might be all over. "Maybe it's just the window that's closed," Draggor said to Alkali as they watched Serathin continue to look around for some way in, the imp putting his hands up to his mouth to try and project his voice. "Serathin, keep trying to find a way in, we're going to try the door!"

The sabrewolf just nodded down to them as the two ran over to the other side of the building and made their way to the entrance. The door was locked and there were a number of buzzers that were on the metal box beside it, but as Alkali tried to figure out which one might have been the number Draggor took the direct route and smashed the glass in with his elbow. Once they had cleared the glass from the frame the two continued their way in and ran up the hallway, not bothering to silence themselves as they got to the stairwell. If the python was still alive in there they might get some sign from a locked door and would just have to wait for The Rat to reset the system again, but if they just heard silence…

No, Alkali told himself not to think that way anymore as both of them ran breathlessly up the stairs towards the eighth floor. The security system being active meant that it was likely the one inside perceived a threat and locked everything down, which also meant that he was probably alive. On another note if he had been attacked and had locked down the room before he was killed it was possible that the killer was in there too. Though the latter option was much more gristly it would still keep the ferret from going to prison as they continued to go up.

With the imp being in much better shape he managed to beat the detective up to the eight floor, Draggor racing through the entrance and disappearing out of Alkali's sight. The ferret had to take a few deep breaths before continuing to climb, his adrenaline and investigative instincts driving him to get to his destination. By the time he had gotten to the door himself he saw Draggor standing in front of the one that had the number eight zero four in cheap bronze on the front of it. They banged on the deep purple wood and shouted that they had a pineapple and anchovy pizza for him, but no one responded as Alkali made his way over to it as well.

"This isn't looking good," Draggor said as they looked over at the panting Alkali. "I know it's probably shuttered, but should we take down the door anyway?"

Alkali gave the demon a nod and the imp quickly got to work, taking the satchel that he had hauled up with him and opening it. He pulled out a screwdriver and popped the hinges, opting to take them off by force instead of just unscrewing them all. The rotted wood provided little resistance and both men took a step to the side as it fell to the floor between them. On the other side of it though was what they had feared; a stainless-steel security shutter hung from ceiling to floor with the end latched in to keep anyone from trying to lift it open. Both of them attempted to use force in order to dislodge the barrier but after several attempts it only wavered slightly against their blows.

As Draggor leaned against the shutter in frustration he turned to the side and perked up when he saw something at eye level with him, pushing on the metal as hard as he good to expose as much of the box on the wall that he spotted. "I think that might be the panic button for the door," Draggor pointed out, going back into his bag of tricks and pulling out a mini-crowbar before handing it to Alkali. "You try and keep the gap open as wide as possible and I'll try and get the box off the wall, from there I could rewire it so we don't have to wait for The Rat to come here and do it for us. It's going to cause a big hole but at this point I don't think it matters."

At this point Alkali was beyond caring about property damage and slid the piece of metal where Draggor told him, the two heard the wood of the doorframe already start to splinter as the imp took his screwdriver and wedged it between the metal box and the wall. It didn't take much for the panel to fall off and when he got it off he dropped the screwdriver back in his bag and pulled out a set of tweezers instead. With much more care than the initial extraction the demon carefully pulled two wires out without the ends touching the metal, then carefully rubbed the exposed copper together which caused a spark to pop and the shutter door to unlock. Draggor grinned in triumph at his feat of electrical engineering as Alkali pulled up the solid piece of metal, the imps face falling at what they saw on the other side.

The python whose name the two still didn't know laid sitting in the reclining chair that sat in front of the television, the tan leather heavily stained red as the creature laid motionless and staring at the ceiling. Even without the scales of his neck split into two and crimson spray on the nearby furniture it was clear that the safe cracker was dead, murdered with one swift stroke of a blade to his throat. Blood was still dripping down onto the quickly growing pool of the carpet beneath his body as Draggor moved forward and checked to see if there was any possible sign of life left. Alkali could feel the blood draining from his own face as the imp looked up at him and shook his head, then used his hand to close the unblinking eyes of the python.

A loud bang caused both demon and ferret to jump and realized that Serathin was still trying to force his way in through the window, Draggor going over and unlocking that one as well using the same trick on the other button. As soon as the metal shutter retracted Serathin came in clutching his forearm, a crimson stream dribbling between his fingers as he grimaced in pain. "Thought maybe I could break the glass and try to go from the top down," the draconic sabrewolf said as he held up his arm, fingers still dripping slightly with blood before it matted his fur down.

"Looks like you're bleeding pretty bad," Draggor said as he gently lifted the hybrid's hand to see the sizable gash in his forearm as they walked over the broken glass on the carpet towards the kitchen.

"Could be worse," Serathin replied, his green eyes glancing over at the dead python that was only a few feet away. "Much worse, it seems. Don't suppose you had a chance to interrogate him and then he did himself in."

"Came in that way," Draggor said as he looked back over at the body. "Blood's still fresh, wound is dripping, couldn't have been more than a few minutes before he died. Looks like the blade that's in his hand was what was used."

Alkali's head felt like it was swimming, the raw coppery smell filling his nostrils as he went in to get his assessment of the scene. Even though he had come to yet another literal dead end there weren't any police chasing him this time, and with it being so late it would be unlikely that anyone would call them. This may have been the chance he had to finally get a bead on the killer, and from the way things were staged it appeared that they were in a hurry as well. The black metal blade that was in the hand of the python looked like it was the same as the one that had been presented as the murder weapon to him in the police station, and with no note and such a messy scene the idea that this was another suicide was laughable.

For what felt like the first time that night Alkali could feel his detective instincts returning back in full force, his mind sharpened like the blade in the python's hand as he knelt down to look at the body. The killer must have seen them coming, maybe from the window, and had to escape quickly. After killing the safe cracker they probably started to put everything in place before he was interrupted, perhaps by Serathin walking up the fire escape towards the window. There were separate panic buttons for the door and windows so they probably activated that one first to keep the hybrid from getting in, then knew they had about eight floors worth of climbing time to get as much as they could set before running out and activating the door before they slipped out and ran to the opposite side of the building.

Missed them by minutes… the words of the demon echoed in Alkali's ears as he began to pace slightly around the body. "He was probably standing somewhere around here when he caught the python by surprise," Alkali said out loud as he mimicked where the killer would have stood. "That way he wouldn't get caught in the spray in order to try and make it look like a third suicide."

"So you're definitely thinking that the killer was here?" Draggor said while directing Serathin to raise his arm up slightly. It appeared the imp had found a medical bag complete with supplies to stitch a wound, which is what he did with the hybrid as he winced in pain.

"Without a doubt," Alkali replied as he continued to look over the knife.

"I'll take your word for it," Serathin said between grimaces. "Although just because his throat is slit like that FBI agent doesn't mean it's our killer, could just be a coincidence."

"It's the same type of blade too," Alkali responded. "Our killer has a fondness for this knife, that could be helpful in narrowing it down. But what's strange is how gruesome this murder is compared to the others, the other two I could believe might have been suicides but this one is just way too messy when there are far easier and cleaner means."

"Well you keep looking around while I make sure our friend here keeps the use of his arm," Draggor said, chuckling when he saw the sabrewolf's eyes go wide. "I'm just kidding, you're just going to be very uncomfortable for a while but you shouldn't lose any motor function."

As Draggor continued to reassure the nervous looking hybrid Alkali decided to take the imp's advice to heart and look around the apartment. There were a number of television cameras and other devices that were set up in the bedroom, but when he attempted to look at the tape he found none was inside. That would have made this a lot easier, the detective thought to himself as he went from the bedroom back to the kitchen. Whomever knew about this python probably guessed that he had some sort of insomnia and that ambushing him in the living room was far easier than doing so in the bedroom where everything was heavily monitored.

When Alkali got to the table however there was something else that caught his interest enough to call the other two over while Draggor continued to bandage Serathin's arm. "Whoa, those are some detailed specs," Serathin said as they all looked down at the blueprint of a large safe vault. "These are very in-depth, more than even manufacturer's prints, are you sure that Poker wasn't actually about to try and rob the vault for real?"

The words hit the ferret right in his investigative gut and it almost knocked the wind out of him. For most of this he had been operating under the assumption that Poker was trying to infiltrate the Kage Syndicate by getting their attention with a fake heist, but what if the FBI agent had been planning it for real? It would have been the perfect cover; if the heist succeeded then the wolf and his team would be off sipping mai tai's on some tropical island away from this frozen forsaken city, but if it failed then he could just say that it was all a ruse sanctioned by the government in order to try and dismantle a powerful crime family. Initially the thought had occurred to Alkali that perhaps he was a rogue FBI agent, but when he was killed he just came to the conclusion that the op he was running was in fact legit.

One problem at a time, Alkali reminded himself. With less than a day on the clock he had to give the Kage Syndicate someone to take to the feds, and so far every good lead and possible suspect ended up dead. Perhaps he could pass off the suicides as signs of guilt, but if he did that than the real killer would go free with four, possibly five bodies on their hands. When Draggor asked what they were supposed to do now the detective didn't have an answer; he had all these pieces with no spaces to fit them in and a bunch of spaces that no piece will fit. He realized at this point that there was one thing that he had with this crime scene that he didn't have with any of the others.

The bodies.

As Alkali took out his watch and looked at it he saw that it was almost four in the morning before putting it back in his breast pocket. He informed the other two that there wasn't going to be anything more that they were going to find there and to wait at the Foxhole for him in the morning. Once the three of them were gone they would call the police and let them pick up yet another body, though as they did Serathin began to freak out about his blood being on the floor at the scene of a potential murder. At this point though there was nothing that they could really do about it and unless the sabrewolf got caught and tested the blood meant nothing to police officers anyway.

The three quickly exited the building and made their way over to where Pandez waited for them, getting inside the truck and being driven to their respective destinations. Instead of giving directions to Xander's apartment Alkali told him to drop him off at a twenty-four hour diner instead, the ferret waving good bye to them once he had disembarked before heading inside. When he walked inside the sudden influx of heat caused his jacket to steam as he looked around at the others who were there. Aside from two drunks that were practically passed out, a homeless man trying not to freeze, and two men who were probably on some third shift job the place was practically empty. That was exactly what he was looking for as he went to the back and used their phone to make a call.

About half an hour later Alkali sat at the booth near the front of the diner, an empty plate the only thing left of either a very late dinner or very early breakfast. The two workers had left to go home by that point and he seemed to be the only conscious person left inside aside from the workers themselves. As he looked out the window and saw the darkness of the night slowly shift into the light of morning he saw a single car drive down the street and make its way towards the diner. Alkali slowly stirred his coffee, which was actually fairly decent at this place, and waited to see who would possibly come through those doors.

A few minutes after the car parked in the lot next to the building a dinosaur man in a white coat came in, looked around for a bit, then noticed Alkali and went over towards him. "Thanks for meeting me on such short notice," Alkali said as the other man sat down opposite him. "I know that it's probably very early for you and I hope I didn't wake you Iggy."

"That's Doctor Iggy to you," The dino said sternly, his face solid before it cracked with a hint of a smile. "You didn't wake me from anything, most nights during the cold snap I got to go out and haul some icicle back to the morgue for storage. Freezer's almost full and I can't exactly just store them outside, but I'm guessing you aren't here to talk shop."

"Well technically I am," Alkali replied, his face falling slightly as he tapped the side of his cup with his spoon. "You've heard about the unpleasant situation that I'm in?"

"It's a bit hard to not hear about it when your assumed handiwork is on my table," Iggy explained. "Don't forget that I'm servicing practically the entire city with all these budget cuts going on, anything more severe than a heart attack and I'm called to examine it. Naturally I don't believe it, but it's hard to keep a straight face when I saw that body come in and they said that you had a hand in his demise."

"It's actually your versatility that I'm hoping to utilize," Alkali said as he leaned in. "What can you tell me about Poker's death?"

"Hey, this isn't some interview for your boyfriend or anything, I could get in real trouble for sharing that information with you," Iggy said, though as Alkali continued to give him a stern look the dino sighed and shook his head. "You're lucky we go way back and you helped me out with that thing; anyway Agent Poker Wolf has suffered a blow to the head and also had received significant trauma damage across his neck and trachea. Cause of death ruled to be exsanguination."

"I see," Alkali stated simply. "Was a full autopsy performed?"

"I think the giant hole in the wolf's neck was proof positive enough," Iggy replied, though once more his cocksure resolve dissolved under the stare of the ferret. "Look, I wanted to dive deeper but the higher-ups overruled me, and before you ask it was the same with those two suicides too. There's no way that I can do anything with those bodies unless I have reasonable cause or something specific I'm looking for."

"Something specific…" Alkali said as he tapped a finger to his lip. "How specific are we talking about here?"

"As in you can name the actual cause of death and I would just be confirming," Iggy quickly explained. "And I only get one bite at the apple, so if you do have something make sure that you know it for certain."

Iggy watched in slight surprise as the ferret seemed to try and think real hard about something, banging his fists to his head a few times before sighing in exacerbation. "It's on the tip of my tongue, but I was in a bit of a rush so I didn't pay too much attention," Alkali sated mostly to himself before looking up at Iggy. "Look, if I can tell you what to test for how long would it take to do it?"

"Probably about… two hours if I'm close to the morgue where the body is?" Iggy guessed.

"Great, try to stay near your phone at the morgue if you can," Alkali said as he got up from his seat and laid a few bills down on the table. "I'm going to get that test name for you as soon as possible."

Alkali got up and left the confused dinosaur sitting there before starting to walk towards the nearest bus stop. He didn't know the number for the bootlegger and didn't have a car of his own, which meant he would need to risk the public exposure in order to try and find what he needed to find. He felt like a dog on the scent of his prey, though he was one on a time limit as he looked at his watch to see it was almost six. Eighteen hours left, with two to run the test and one to capture the killer, it was going to be close but with the new information in his head the shadowy figure became a little clearer.

Eventually the bus managed to get him to where he needed to go, Alkali standing in front of the familiar produce packing facility that he had visited before. He knew that it would be likely that those who worked inside would recognize him from their previous encounter, but all he needed was a name and he could escape. There was even a route he could take to make a quick getaway even if it was the South River as he moved swiftly between the conveyor belts towards the back office. It didn't take long before the stares of recognition began to come his way with one bull in particular dropping his clipboard before running towards the shipping area of the plant.

It would still be several minutes after the call was placed for the police to arrive, Alkali thought to himself as he quickened his pace, and that was if they made the trespassing a priority. He guessed that he probably had ten minutes and glanced at his watch to keep time so he didn't overstay his welcome. The entire walk to the back offices only took three minutes and the climb up the stairs was one as the ferret saw the door he was aiming for crisscrossed with yellow police tape. Several of the office workers poked their heads out only to quickly dart back inside and lock their doors when they saw who was there, but the ferret paid them no mind as he attempted to open the office of the district manager.

When Alkali found it was locked he decided to go the direct route and slammed his foot against the door, causing the glass to shatter and the remaining frame to swing open as shouts could be heard on the plant floor. Add another crime to the rap sheet, he thought to himself, but if this helped proofed that he didn't commit murder then he would be happy to serve the extra days in jail. As he looked around the office he had broken into however he felt himself swallow hard as most of the things that were on the bull's desk were gone. No way… Alkali's eyes twitched slightly as they looked over the empty tables on the side of the wall as he realized that the police had taken everything from the room and had put it into evidence.

Alkali could hear the shouts of others coming from the plant and with the information he needed not where he thought it was the ferret quickly made his way out of the plant before the police arrived or the workers took matters into their own hands. This time he left with plenty of time to spare before the cops arrived and walked his way through the frigid city streets until he could catch a bus back to Xander's place. Other than letting the dragon know that he was alright he also needed to sleep if he was going to make a final push to make Uncle Kage's deadline. Before he crashed on the bed though he made a call to Zen to make sure that Trinity was going to be at the speakeasy that night…

Chapter Nine – Compiling the Evidence

The sun went down on the city as Alkali made his way out from the pool hall he had been hiding out in as the temperatures dipped below freezing once more. For the ferret it was almost ominous that such a chill would set in when it was potentially his last night as a free man. He knew that if he didn't find a killer within the next four hours the Kage Syndicate would serve him up to the FBI, and while he had an idea on the matter of suspects the problem was that there wasn't enough evidence to satisfy the cockroach. Everything rode on this last gambit and it would involve going into the lion's den itself as he made his way to the speakeasy.

With it being so close to the deadline Alkali opted to go in through the back door instead of the front, and as he did he gave a small nod to the panda bootlegger that was there. He had once more managed to coerce Pandez into carting him around where he would need to go next, though he knew that he wouldn't like the destination. Something told him that perhaps Trinity had leaned on him a little bit in order to help out, though that would have caused her to potentially compromise her cover. With a killer on the loose and one federal agent dead along with three others perhaps she thought that catching them was more important than breaking a bootleg booze ring or whatever else she had been trying to do.

As the ferret got inside the bar he could see that Trinity was singing on stage, an indicator that she was at least still undercover within the speakeasy. He also saw Zen behind the bar talking with Xander, Draggor, and Serathin as he served them drinks. "Looks like the gang's all here," Alkali said as he went over and sat down next to them. "Did Zen tell you what the plan was?"

"Only that you're going to be doing something incredibly stupid," Draggor responded. "The only way that I'm going to link all these murders together and figure out what's happening is to get those evidence reports from the police station. I need to know what was in the office of that bull so that I can get the information to my friend."

"So you're going to just go break into the police station," Xander stated with a huff. "Why don't you let me try to use my press credentials to get the information you need? I'm sure I can figure out what you're looking for if you just tell me what it is."

Alkali shook his head at that, trying not to tip his hat on the information he was actually looking for to the group. "I have less than four hours before the entire Kage Syndicate falls on my head," Alkali replied. "Going through proper credentials is going to take way longer than the time I have left, and I don't think Kage is going to appreciate me being late. Fortunately the logs that I want aren't in the station that I escaped so they probably won't be looking for me."

"Doesn't mean that they're not going to lock you up if they find you," Serathin said, a small grin on his muzzle. "I like it though, a bold and daring move in the eleventh hour. Are we going to be sneaking in again together?"

"Actually… I'm thinking about bringing someone who isn't a criminal," Alkali replied as the demon and hybrid looked at one another while Zen chuckled, only for the fox to stop as the detective looked up on the stage. "I'm going to need to borrow Trinity from you for a few hours, you're going to have to entertain the drunks in some other fashion."

All four of the others were shocked that Alkali mentioned the wolfdog as they turned their head to look at the singer, but before any of them could say anything Zen asked for the others to give him and the ferret a few seconds to talk in private. Though it looked like the other three wanted to say something they were quickly hushed by the fox and then told to give them some space. Alkali watched them quickly get the hint and make their way to the other side of the speakeasy even though only a few feet of space would have been enough. Alkali could feel the cold stare of the bartender on him already as he found a glass suddenly put in front of him.

"Are you sure that you want her?" Zen asked once they were sure that none of the others could hear them.

"I figure it would be good to have an ATF agent on my side in case we get caught," Alkali replied, unable to hold back his smirk as he watched the look of surprise on the fox's face. "I already know who she is Zen, and I'm also pretty certain that you already knew that too."

Zen's mouth opened and shut a few times with no words coming out until finally he let out a small chuckle. "I should have known that you would have figured it out sooner or later," Zen stated. "Listen, I hear that they're already thinking about overturning prohibition and if that's the case then this sewer swill isn't going to cut it anymore. Someone comes by and offers to buy you out in exchange for setting up a sting in your place and you take the money."

So, the gala heist had just been something that she just stumbled upon, Alkali thought to himself as a wave of relief cascaded through him that coincided with the shot of liquor he took. While he was pretty sure that Trinity had been telling him the truth the entire time this just confirmed it as the fox shook his head. It was hard to find people to trust in this city and harder still to keep them, and if he was going to break into another evidence locker he wanted someone that he was sure would have his back. The fact that she hadn't arrested him already meant that she was on his side… at last until the Kage Syndicate turned him over to the feds.

Just as he had that thought he suddenly noticed there were several Alkali recognized as part of the Syndicate that came into the speakeasy. Unlike the others that he had seen in the bar though this group clearly were looking for something, or more likely someone as they scoped the area. The ferret took out his pocket watch and looked at the time before he started to move towards the stage. He wasn't sure who they wanted but he didn't want it to be him, unfortunately as he made his way through the makeshift dance floor he suddenly heard a shout and turned to see the group of four looking at him.

The noise was enough to stop both Trinity and the band that had been playing, an eerie silence filling the room as Alkali faced the ones that had gotten everyone's attention. It felt like he had just said a curse word in church as everyone who wasn't a part of the group backed away to give the four guys that came in some space. "Should have known that you would be in one of these places," the leader of the group said, the armadillo adjusting his hat as well as the overcoat that hung from his shoulders. "You going to come with us quietly or are we going to have a little dance of our own on that thick skull of yours?"

"What are you talking about?" Alkali asked, every nerve in his body telling him that he was in danger as the other three began to clear out the speakeasy while the leader stared at him with a sneer. "Kage said that I have twenty-four hours and there's still three hours before midnight. It's not like him to suddenly be impatient."

"You must have heard him wrong," the armadillo said, drawing his revolver and causing a few panicked cries to come up from the thinning crowd. "You're out of time detective, now if you have the name of the one that you say set you up then you can tell the boss when you go to meet him. If you resist though then you won't be able to say anything, since we'll be bringing in a corpse."

Despite trying to put on a tough act he found himself swallowing hard at the threat. They had enough to pin the murder of Agent Poker Wolf on him and since he had escaped custody he was technically a fugitive. But he also still didn't have enough evidence to point Kage in the direction of the real killer, especially if it's the one that was at the top of his list. But with the gangsters not accepting that he still had a few hours left on the clock his immediate need was to escape by any means necessary, unfortunately with the armadillo having the gun on him there was nothing that he or the rest of his group watching could do without risking him getting shot.

As Alkali pondered his options the leader of the group got visibly angry and moved towards him, keeping the gun pointed at his head while grabbing him by the coat. The armadillo told him to move it and spun him around so that he was between Alkali and the back exit as the other three moved forward to clear a path for them. It was then the ferret found his possible means of escape and pretended to trip to fall forward against one of the potted plants that were spread about the speakeasy. The greenery wasn't just to make the place look nice as he looked down at the mixture of silica dust and charcoal powder, a mixture that specialized in neutralizing alcohol so people could dump their drinks into the pots and avoid being arrested.

Alkali had a different idea for the powder however as he grabbed a fistful and quickly spun around before throwing it directly into the armadillo's eyes. The gangster let out a howl of pain as the ferret followed up by taking a nearby chair and smashing it into the guy before he ran for the back exit. A gunshot rang through the air like a crack of thunder as the blind armadillo fired wildly as the rest of his gang turned and drew their weapons as well. The exit was too far away for the ferret to get at before they drew on him so he went for the next best thing, which was a barrier between him and the ones that pulled out lugers and pistols of their own. As the ferret jumped over one of the metal tables he grabbed the back edge of it and knocked it down behind him.

The heavy sound of metal hitting metal rang in Alkali's ears as bullets fell on his makeshift shield like lead raindrops. The table wouldn't last very long under that assault but he knew the second that he moved out of its safety they would be able to shoot him. As he thought about what to do he heard more gunshots, but this time it came from his side of the stage. The bouncing of metal against the table ceased briefly and when he looked out from behind it he saw the three gang members scrambling for cover.

The window of opportunity gave Alkali a chance to make a run for it and as he did he saw Draggor and Zen both firing weapons of their own, the imp with a streetsweeper while the fox fired off shells from his shotgun at the group. "Last call!" Zen shouted as he ducked behind the bar just as two of the gangsters recovered and fired on him and began to shatter the bottles behind him. "You might want to run that errand while you have the chance Alkali!"

Alkali didn't have to be asked twice in order to make a run for it, hearing the rattling of Draggor's tommy gun to keep the four gang members occupied. Even with the cover fire the ferret heard several bullets whiz over his head as he squeezed off a few rounds of his own before he got to the back door and flung it open. When he got to the other side he saw Trinity there, the wolfdog pulling him into the alleyway before slamming it shut behind him. The sound of bullets hitting the door could be heard on the other side as the shootout at the speakeasy continued within.

As Trinity and Alkali made their way down the alley they suddenly heard more shouting and the ferret turned to see several more members of the Kage syndicate at the entrance to the alley. The two of them turned and ran back towards the bootlegger car with the panda looking up after putting the last small cask on a pile. Alkali shouted at Pandez to get the car started and he did so, the engine roaring over the sound of commotion that came from the group that ran down towards them. There was an another exit to the alley besides the one filled with people armed with guns, but it would take a second to get it turned around and already they were starting to fire at them. One of the bullets hit the barrel near the ferret and just as he was about to pass by it he stopped and got an idea.

"Alkali, this is no time for a drink!" Trinity shouted as she hopped on the back of the truck while it maneuvered its way to face the exit. The ferret just grabbed the already leaking barrel and tossed it into the alley. He could hear Pandez shout something about alcohol abuse as he tossed two more before he ran back towards the truck as well.

The sound of glass breaking could be heard as Alkali got into the back of the truck as well, Pandez ducking down as several bullets hit the windshield and side windows. By that point though the panda had managed to navigate his way to the alley. As they started to drive down Alkali poked his head out from the trailer of the truck and saw the gangsters were about to cross over the increasing puddle of liquor. The detective pointed his weapon and fired several shots, but instead of aiming at any of the gangsters he fired on the wet concrete.

One of the bullets sparked as it hit and that was enough to ignite the moonshine, causing the group to cry out and fall back as a fireball engulfed the entirety of the alley. "There, that should stop them," Alkali said with a grin as he watched the men fall back, though his face fell as he saw the fire trace back to the small pile of barrels that were stacked up. He darted over and brought Trinity, who had just poked her head up to see the commotion, to the floor of the truck as the fires licked around the wood of the bathtub gin and caused them to explode.

The truck's back tires lifted up slightly from the force of the explosion before it bounced back down. When both Trinity and Alkali looked up from the truck they saw the new fireball rise up into the sky as sirens began to blare in the distance. "I hope you didn't need to go back there anytime soon," Trinity said before she went up to the front wall and opened the door. "You alright up there Pandez?"

"Yeah, can't say the same for my poor truck," Pandez replied forlornly as he looked at the holes in his windshield. "By the way, did you just blow up the entire stash of booze I delivered back there?"

"Zen wasn't going to need it anyway," Alkali replied dismissively before he looked at his watch. "We're going to have to hurry, even if that group jumped the gun I'm going to find one pointed at me in about three hours."

About twenty minutes later Pandez brought Trinity and Alkali to the police station that handled the jurisdiction where Miles had been killed. It was the last place where any of them wanted to be but the ferret knew that the information that would lead him to concrete evidence on who killed Agent Poker as well as the others was inside. The rum runner dropped them off about a block away, not wanting to take a bullet-riddled car right up to the cops, and bid them a fond farewell. Trinity stepped up onto the door of the truck and hugged him, which caused him to blush before he drove off.

Once they had waved off the truck Trinity and Alkali turned back and made their way towards the police station. The freezing temperature did little to help the nerves that the detective felt as he made his way towards a place that should have at least been a neutral ground for him. While the cops didn't appreciate him sticking his muzzle into their business occasionally at least they were somewhat on the same side, but this time he was going in as an enemy. It was hard for him to believe that less than two days ago he had escaped from one only to walk back in now.

"You know that even with my credentials I'm not going to be able to save you if they find out you're a fugitive," Trinity explained as they got into the shelter of a nearby building to keep warm while they scoped the police station out. It stood there like a fortress and almost seemed to be daring him to step inside. "The last two and a half hours of freedom that you have will be spent inside a prison cell before they ship you off."

"I understand," Alkali replied as he sighed and leaned against the brick wall for support. "If you don't want to do this I can try and get in myself, last thing I need is for you to blow up your career to help me out. Might be better if you turned around and walked back out of here, put me and this whole situation in your rear view."

"At this point it would be more detrimental for me to leave now," Trinity replied with a light laugh. "My entire investigation is in shambles and if the department found out I let a murderer who killed an agent and three others go free they would run me right out on the rails. Now let's just not get caught sneaking in and I won't have to use my identification."

Even though the indication that this was all strictly business Alkali could sense that the wolfdog seemed genuinely concerned for his wellbeing. It was hard for the ferret to believe that the speakeasy singer that came in through his door asking for help was by his side checking on her pistol before putting it back into her coat. When he saw that she noticed him looking at her the detective quickly averted his gaze to the pocket watch he had pulled out of his breast pocket to look at the time. Two and a half hours… this was going to cut it real close and it was unlikely the cockroach would be in a good mood towards him considering the shootout they had just gone through.

Once they had significantly warmed themselves up enough to endure more time out in the cold the two made their way out of the laundromat they had holed up in and moved towards the police station itself. Most of the building was surrounded by a barbed-wire fence that Alkali didn't have the means to bypass, which meant they were going to have to take the much riskier motorpool entrance. They got to the edge of the garage and waited for about a minute before they headed towards the smaller employee door that was next to the big one for the cars to enter and exit. Just as Alkali was about to pull out his lockpick set however they heard the grinding of gears and both he and Trinity ducked to a small frost-covered shrub in an attempt to hide themselves.

Alkali froze more than the cold air that he had drawn into his lungs before he held his breath and waited. If someone had seen them sneak up towards the garage entrance than their incursion would be over before it started, but as they watched they saw the patrol car slowly drive out and onto the street. When the vehicle had turned the corner and disappeared the ferret looked back to the garage as the door remained open, realizing they had an opportunity to breach the station with minimal effort. He got the wolfdog's attention and the two of them darted forward to get inside before someone came to close the door on them.

The two just managed to get inside and behind a different squad car as they saw a horse man in a uniform come out from the station and walk towards the door while muttering about the cold and how he wished they would keep the garage closed. Once more the two remained still and watched as he went over and pulled the cord that brought the metal door down with a loud slam, then walked back towards the station. Though they had successfully gotten in that was the least of their problems at the moment, even with it being the night shift it had taken a call for an officer down to empty the station that allowed Alkali to get into evidence and claim his personal items. He had no such means to do the same and that meant there were far more eyes inside than the last time he did this.

Once they had made sure the bull wouldn't come back Alkali and Trinity carefully crept their way forward and went up to the door that divided the motorpool from the station. With the blood pounding in his ears it made it hard for the detective to hear if there was anyone on the other side, but when he heard nothing he decided to risk it and slowly open the door. They only opened it a crack and saw that the hallway was completely empty aside from a few boxes and a plant in desperate need of watering. With the coast clear they made their way inside and slowly closed the door behind them before they moved froward.

When they got to the end of the hallway they saw the standard bullpen that police stations had with the horse officer they had seen earlier sitting at his desk reading a book. With it being as cold as it was it was unlikely the streets were filled with crime and those that weren't relegating to patrolling the streets probably had a boring night ahead of them. Anything that took their attention away from their surroundings was a good thing though as they moved forward towards the detective offices. They had too stop more than once when they saw other cops milling about, grabbing coffee or just walking to stretch their legs. As they got to the other end of the room Alkali noticed that one of them was a racoon-husky hybrid that he thought worked for the station that had initially arrested him… but there wasn't time to satiate his curiosity as they ducked back around another corner.

As they had thought all the detectives had already gone home for the day, which left the area with their offices completely deserted and allowed for easier access to the rest of the building. Though Alkali hadn't visited this particular station the layouts were fairly similar to one another and he knew that from the detective's hallway it linked to the reporting desk and then evidence lockup. The evidence room was not their actual target though; most of time it had someone stationed there and if it didn't then the security was much harder to get into than the standard locks, and he doubted that his lockpicking skills were on par with the sneak thief that had gotten him in there in the first place. Fortunately all the evidence would be written up and put in the case file that was in the records room that the two went towards.

The door opened with a soft click as the two went inside, then closed the door behind them and looked around. Alkali was about to lock it when he thought better of it; better for them to hear it open and have a chance to hide rather than an officer becoming immediately suspicious upon finding it mysteriously locked. Since the case was less than a week old the folder for it likely wouldn't have been filed in the cabinets yet, even if they did rule it a suicide and closed the case. As he looked at the pile of papers on the receiving desk though he frowned at the disorganization of dozens of folders with only one containing the information that he needed. There was nothing that they could do however but search it as they went over and began to comb through them looking for the name of the one they were looking for.

After about fifteen minutes Alkali sat back on the chair with a hasty pile of folders stacked up next to him. He had split the work with Trinity and had managed to finish his first as he rubbed his face with his hands. He had been dry on his search and if it wasn't with the hybrid than it was possible one of the detectives had it, or more likely it was at the bullpen of one of the unfortunate rookies that it got pawned off on in order to finish out the paper work. "Looks like you had just as much luck as I did Momma T," Alkali said as the wolfdog slammed the last folder down in exasperation while shaking her head. "Great… there's no way that we're going to sneak around that bullpen even if they are all distracted, and unless we go to their equipment room and steal a radio we can't call anything out that will have them evacuate the building."

"What about a fire alarm?" Trinity suggested. "We pull that and search the area while they evacuate."

"It's standard procedure to lock everything up before they leave if they can," Alkali replied. "Plus they would probably do a quick sweep to try and find the source of the fire if they could and try to put it out themselves. We could try a bribe but I don't have much left after paying our bootlegger, and if they know who I am that doesn't work either."

As Alkali listed all the options that wouldn't work for this particular scenario it failed to manifest one that would, the two sitting in silence save for the hum of the electric lights overhead and ticking of the nearby clock. Without even looking at it the ferret knew that his time was almost up and if he aborted this operation he probably wouldn't have a chance to set anything else up. His options now were to give himself up to the police and hope that Boozy could mitigate the damages, or he would have to start running now and hope that he could outwit the entire Kage Syndicate. Maybe he could hide out in one of those distillery dens out in the woods, at least he could drink his problems away before he got caught.

The two had been so engrossed in their problem that they didn't even realize that someone was at the door before it had closed behind them. The two practically jumped up as they saw the jaguar standing there with a look of confusion on his face, his fingers gripped against the paper of a folder that he was probably about to add to the stack that were in front of them. "Who… who are you two?" the feline asked, his eyes darting between the two unexpected people in the room he had believed to be empty.

It was clear that this guy, hardly more than a kid, was a rookie to the force. That was a relief in that he not only didn't recognize Alkali as a detective but also as a fugitive. This fact gave them options on how to proceed with the encounter, but they still had to explain why they were in the records room of a police station uninvited. The detective looked into the eyes of the officer and could tell that his thoughts were quickly guiding him to drop the file and make a grab for his gun, and though he and Trinity could probably outdraw him the last thing they needed was a shootout at a police station.

Before the jaguar could do anything Trinty stepped forward with a calm, resigned look on her face and pulled out her identification. "I'm Agent Trinity, ATF," she said as she held the badge in front of the officer's face. "I'm working a joint operation with your station in order to break the bootleg booze ring that's been plaguing your district for quite some time."

"ATF?" The jaguar repeated, the wolfdog giving him a nod in affirmation. "They didn't tell any of us about this."

"That's because it's believed that there might be someone tipping these gin jockeys when potential raids are going to happen," Trinity explained with such a certainty that Alkali almost believed it. "Aside from your chief no one knows that we're sharing resources, which is why we decided to come here at night. Tell me, what's your name?"

The question had caught the feline slightly off-guard and he gave her a look of surprise before responding. "Oh, uh, Officer Jenkins," the jaguar replied with a hint of excitement in his voice. "So ATF, you guys going after the Kage Syndicate?"

"I'm afraid that information is on a need-to-know basis," Trinity replied quickly. "I can trust that you will be extremely discrete about this information Officer Jenkins, I would hate for a promising career such as yours to be cut short because you couldn't keep your muzzle shut."

"Oh, yes ma'am, I'll be sure to keep this operation a secret," Jenkins replied before his gaze went from Trinity to Alkali. "And who are you sir?" This time it was the ferret's turn to be surprised by the question, but as Trinity looked back at him as well he knew that he couldn't just answer with his own name in case his identity had been shared with other stations. He could feel each second tick by as his mind tried to come up with an answer, wishing desperately at that moment he had something like the wolfdog had he could just flash in order to give himself the same authority…

…or did he already have something like that?

Keeping his composure like an ace detective would Alkali didn't break eye contact as he slid his hand into the inner pocket of his coat. His heart skipped a beat as he found his fingers brush against leather and he quickly pulled out the wallet that was within to show the inquisitive officer. "I'm… Agent Poker Wolf with the FBI," Alkali said as he held out the badge, seeing Trinity's eyes widen slightly as he impersonated an agent right in front of her. "Since the Kage Syndicate is a gang that operates in multiple states obviously we were brought in on the investigation as well."

"Ah, of course, Agent… Wolf?" The jaguar said as he looked the ferret up and down.

"Yes, Wolf," Alkali doubled-down while he gave the feline a stern look. "Do you have a problem with my being raised by wolves?"

"No, of course not sir!" Jenkins replied as he back-pedaled quickly. "I'll just go back to work and make sure no one disturbs you! If you need anything just let me know-"

"Actually…" Trinity interrupted, tapping a finger on her snout as she decided to use their newfound authority to their advantage. "You're new here, aren't you?" The jaguar nodded which prompted them to do the same. "I know it's hard being new, I bet they stick all the boring or tedious cases on you to fill out, right?"

"Well, yeah…" Jenkins said as he rubbed the back of his head.

"We were looking for a file that I think you probably have then," Trinity said as she sat down on the corner of the desk. "It would have been labeled as a suicide, which is why they would have pawned it off on you since it's a boring case with a lot of paperwork attached to it. What they don't know is that it's actually linked to our investigation, and that means that if we find any leads that result from it the officer responsible for the case usually gets a commendation on it."

Clearly the words were something Officer Jenkins wanted to hear as his ears perked up at the mention of a commendation. "Yeah, I can go and get it for you right now!" A small grin played on the edges of Trinity's face as she looked back at Alkali once more, who just gave her a small nod of approval before the voice of the jaguar could be heard getting their attention. "Which suicide case did you want exactly?"

"Which case?" Alkali asked first in slight surprise. "You have more than one?"

Chapter Ten – Making the Arrest

A few minutes later both Trinity and Alkali had a case file in their hands after they found out Officer Jenkins had not only got handed the suicide from the produce sorting facility but also the one from the safehouse apartment. He hadn't realized that the second one was in this district but it was more information at his fingertips, something that up until this point he had been desperately lacking. Once the jaguar had given them both reports they sent him back to his desk to make sure he didn't arouse suspicion by being in the records room for too long. The jaguar seemed slightly disappointed that he couldn't continue to participate on the case but gave them both a nod of understanding and once more told them that he was there to help before he left.

"Feel kind of bad for lying to him," Alkali stated once the cop was gone as he flipped through papers.

"If we catch the killer I'll make sure that he's rewarded for it," Trinity replied. "So did you find what you're looking for, Agent Wolf?"

Trinity snickered at that as Alkali rolled his eyes, but in truth he had just come across the list of evidence that had been taken from the office of Miles. When he got to what he was looking for he put down the file and rolled the chair over to the phone in the room, calling his coroner friend. "Yeah, sorry that it took so long to find the information," Alkali said as he heard the angry mumbling of Iggy on the other end. "Listen, the poison that I need you to test for is for a toxin that comes from the Belladonna plant."

"Nightshade poison?" Iggy asked, though it was more of a statement. "Alright, I'm at the morgue right now with the bodies so I can test them out starting with Agent Wolf and continuing with the others as long as I don't strike out. It's going to be about an hour though before I finish testing all four."

Alkali looked up at the clock and saw that with the test it would pretty much bring him right up to the deadline, but at this point he was sure he wasn't wrong as he told the coroner that was fine and to call him at his office before hanging up. "You think that Poker was poisoned along with being bashed in the head and stabbed?" Trinity asked after the ferret hung up the phone. "That seems like overkill."

"I think that his being poisoned was the reason that everything else happened to him," Alkali admitted, his mind putting together the pieces of the puzzle with the new pieces that had fallen into place. "My guess is that Poker had gotten into my office and had gotten poisoned, and the killer then made it look like he had been murdered in a different fashion in order to cover it up. Had the police found an otherwise perfectly healthy body on the ground they would have ordered a toxin screening for the autopsy, which would have revealed the poison that I believe was used in the other so-called suicides as well except for the python."

"So… Poker was poisoned after going into your office…" Trinity said slowly as she caught up to where Alkali was in the case. "But that means…"

"Agent Poker wasn't the killer's main target," Alkali said as the reality of the situation settled in his stomach like a brick. "I was."

Even though he had already come to that conclusion the detective shivered when the words left his lips. This entire time they were tracking someone that they thought had gone after an FBI agent when in reality they were after someone else, a detective that had gotten himself mixed up in all this in the first place. While he couldn't quite piece together why the killer would want him out of the way it was the only thing that made sense, otherwise why would they try to obfuscate the fact that the wolf had been poisoned in his office? In fact the deaths of the other three might have been a direct result of the mix-up, a thought he shared with Trinity as he put the folder down on the table.

"Well, this is great news, right?" Trinity said once Alkali had finished his musing. "That means you're off the hook, you can tell

Uncle Kage what happened and he can get his Syndicate to back off."

"Not quite," Alkali replied with a sigh. "All I did was figure out that I was the target, and though I have a decent idea of who did it there's no way that I can prove it yet without determining the why. Speaking of such things did you get any information on the file of the one we visited?"

The wolfdog had been looking down at the desk in contemplation until she realized she had been asked a question, then looked at the file in her hand. "The police arrived on the scene and found the deceased in his chair with one of his kitchen knives in his hand, death ruled suicide by exsanguination. They did log the blueprints for the vault but they didn't believe there was enough there to connect it to anything in particular and pawned the case off on Officer Jenkins, didn't see any Belladonna plants listed either."

There wouldn't be any plants at his apartment, Alkali thought to himself as Trinity unknowingly handed him a clue to his case. He looked up at the clock once more and found that there was only forty-seven minutes left until his time was up, and though a plan formed in his mind he didn't like it at all. It was the only way they were going to get enough evidence to catch the killer as he got up from the desk and began to walk towards the door. When Trinity looked at him in confusion the ferret told her that he would explain along the way before the two quietly snuck out of the station and back between the spires of the city.

Despite the Syndicate and police potentially looking for him Alkali and Trinity traveled by taxi back to Alkali's office. It felt strange to the detective to go back to where everything started, feeling a bit like he was returning to the scene of the crime as they were dropped off. When he looked up he saw that the lights in his office were off and everything appeared to be quiet within. The ferret sighed deeply, his breath crystalizing into a cloud that he brought his watch through in order to see he had less than ten minutes before midnight.

"Are you sure you don't want me to go in with you?" Trinity said as they both got out of the cab and stood on the icy sidewalk.

"I'll be fine," Alkali replied. "I just need to go and find one thing before we head to the Kage Syndicate to clear my name, you stay here and make sure that the cab is ready for when I get out." The wolfdog nodded and wished him good luck before turning and getting back into the cab while Alkali moved forward into his building. As he approached the door to the communal hallway time seemed to be moving paradoxically fast and slow at the same time, the seconds draining away while everything seemed to be happening in slow motion.

Don't have time to worry, Alkali reminded himself as he went up the stairs until he reached the floor of his office. As soon as he got there he could see his broken door was bolted shut and sectioned off by police tape to indicate it was still a crime scene. Disturbing it would be one more crime that he could add to his list during these forty-eight hours as he walked right up to it and kicked it in, breaking the already damaged frame and causing the window that bared his name and occupation to shatter. Subtlety was not a luxury that he could afford as he went over to his desk and sat down just in time to hear his phone ring.

While he hadn't been exactly sure who was about to be on the line as he sat in the dark recess of his former sanctuary Alkali was relieved to find Iggy's voice on the other end. "So I tested all four of the corpses that were brought in today," the coroner explained. "Agent Poker and two others did test positive for Nightshade poisoning, but the python didn't have any in his system."

"No, I suppose he wouldn't," Alkali replied, then cut off Iggy before he could ask why. "Thanks, you've been a huge help."

Alkali hung up the phone and leaned back in his chair for a few seconds before he slid down on his hands and knees to look underneath his desk. He had thought all the way back to the box of evidence that had been collected from his place and had realized there was something that had been missing from it, a key piece of evidence that had likely gone unobserved due to the fact that they had found what they thought was the murder weapon in his desk. What they didn't know was that the real one had been pushed or kicked underneath it, a small grin on Alkali's face as he saw the glint of glass under one of the wooden legs. He carefully reached out and grabbed the small glass, the one that Poker had drank out of and then knocked over when the effects of the poison kicked in.

Just as he had gotten back up and put the glass down on the table Alkali heard the door to his bedroom squeak as he saw the movement in the shadows. Alkali reached for his gun but before he could bring up his arm to fire something hit him in his chest that caused his entire body to freeze. The dull thud echoed in his ears as he looked down and saw the knife that stuck out from his chest right over his heart, time slowing down as the handle of the black blade wiggled slightly from the impact. A red stain immediately began to wet the edges of his shirt as a sharp pain suddenly radiated from the spot that caused him to groan.

Everything flashed before the detective's eyes as the entire world grew darker, the shock of the wound seeping into his brain as time slowed down to a crawl. Everything about the last three days flashed before his eyes and he could finally see what happened while he was in his office. He even saw how Poker died, watching the wolf take a drink of his tequila before he began to choke as the poison took effect, then fell forward as his head bounced off the corner of his desk. As he watched the end of the wolf's life play out before him it made him wonder if this was his time as he felt his body start to grow chilled, freezing like the city he had tried to survive in for the last few days.

With his eyes glued to the knife that had buried itself in his flesh he was only vaguely aware of someone moving around him as a heat began to accompany the pain that came from his chest. "Huh, still alive…" the voice next to him said as Alkali's body tingled, the shock of being stabbed setting in as his brain tried to get his body to respond only to feel the gun get ripped out of his hands. "Perhaps I'm getting a little rusty with my throwing skills, too used to being up close and personal. Of course that just means that I can stage something a little more believable thanks to the snake venom that I coated the blade with after running out of nightshade."

So that's why he couldn't move, Alkali thought to himself as he found himself unable to bring up his head or move his limbs. "I should have known," Alkali said as he felt his arms get put onto the armrests of his chair. "Did you wait for me here or were you following me… Serathin…"

Alkali suddenly felt himself get pushed so that his back was against the chair and he was leaning backwards, which allowed him to see the devilish smile on the draconic sabrewolf's face as he looked down at him. "Followed you of course," Serathin replied. "I was really hoping that you had found a dead-end when it came to those files, but when you came here and I overheard your little call with the coroner I knew that you had put it together and would tell Kage everything to try and avoid jail. But I'm guessing an ace detective like you wanted to be sure before you told him, which is why you're forcing me to intervene yet again."

"Just like you intervened with the other members of your crew?" Alkali stated, which caused Serathin's smirk to fall into a frown. "That fourth dossier from Poker's safehouse, that was you right? That's why you burned down the warehouse, you knew from experience where he kept those files, just not the exact location, and after it was revealed he was an FBI agent conducting a sting you couldn't let that fact get out in the open."

"Heh, we knew that he was an FBI agent all along," Serathin said as the grin returned to his muzzle. "It was really quite the perfect plan; the rest of the crew and myself were going to actually rob the gala, and then when the Syndicate looked into it everything would fall on a rogue agent that decided the money was worth more than the job." Alkali suddenly found the hybrid inches from him as the sabrewolf's face contorted briefly into malice. "It was the perfect plan, until Trinity overheard the plan and got YOU involved."

Keep him talking… that was all the detective could think about as he winced from the knife suddenly being removed from his chest. Even though the blade hadn't gotten deep enough to kill him instantly it was still very painful, especially with the venom that continued to keep him in that chair and render him completely immobile. "You were the one thing that I didn't expect when I hijacked Poker's plan," Serathin continued as he looked at the blood-stained blade. "I knew if you were on the case that you would probably figure out what really happened, and since the success of our project depended on Poker being the fall guy I had to make sure you wouldn't be there to solve the case."

"That's where… that's where it all went off the rails, didn't it?" Alkali replied, his vision growing hazy as it felt like someone was pouring needles into his veins. "You poisoned my tequila knowing that I would drink it at some point, but what you didn't expect was that Poker would come here first and help himself. I bet you hid in the same place that you had when you ambushed me… I wish I could have seen your face when you saw that it wasn't me lying on the ground, instead finding you meal ticket on the ground gasping for air."

Though it was clear that what Alkali was saying had started to get under the hybrid's skin that's exactly what he wanted, it wasn't the first time he had come up against someone like this and the one thing he found was that they always wanted to make sure that it's known they're still the best. "I'll admit that Poker being killed had put a wrench in my plans," Serathin admitted through gritted teeth before he gave Alkali a predatory smile. "But like most cats I always land on my feet, and fortunately he was already in position to lay the blame at someone else's."

That was where he came in, Alkali thought bitterly to himself as he remembered the scene vividly in his mind. By this point Serathin had already left out the same escape route he had attempted, something that he showed he could use the fire escape with ease when they went to the Rat safehouse. He probably also called the police on him just before he left to make sure he didn't have a chance to cover it up or run, and with the death of an FBI agent they would have probably just thrown him in jail and thrown away the key. Of course that wouldn't be the case as Uncle Kage had decided to get him out to investigate himself.

"I'm sure it was quite the shock when Uncle Kage called you in to bust me out so I could look into it," Alkali said with a weak chuckle as he watched Serathin examine the gun he had taken from him. "Is that when you decided to kill off the rest of your crew, or were you already planning on doing that? And how did you manage to poison them?"

"At least I didn't get surprised by your early release," Serathin retorted. "The others were unfortunate collateral damage but with Poker dead the heist couldn't happen anyway, so I got up early and while you were at Anthrocon I took the nightshade that Miles had been growing to take out the guards and distilled it into a poison that I slipped into his coffee and the panther's shampoo bottle. They were creatures of habit and we had already known each other for a while so it wasn't hard to time, the only problem came when that stupid python saw me coming and broke schedule to run."

"So that's how you did it," Alkali replied as he imagined the draconic sabrewolf sneaking into their houses and dosing them just like he had described, then slipping in after the poison took hold and making it look like they had killed themselves. "Thief and assassin, or are you just some sort of psychopath that enjoys killing on the side?"

"Hey, it's a down economy, a lot of people have two jobs," Serathin stated with a chuckle as he sat down on the desk with the gun in one hand and his knife in the other. "There is one thing that I have to ask before you die… when did you start suspecting it was me? You didn't know about the poison until just now and even than there was no real link to me except where I smashed your tequila bottle to make sure you went to prison instead of died."

"That was quite the risk to leave that bottle out by the way," Alkali commented. "If I had decided to take a drink or some officer shared it with the department you would have had a lot of problems."

"It was a calculated risk," Serathin replied. "You would have known something was up if the bottle was gone and I had planned on breaking into the station to get my knife back anyway. When I saw it there after you broke into evidence I knew I had to get rid of it in the hopes you would be the scapegoat and sent to prison."

"It was in the safehouse actually, though your theatrics in the evidence locker helped," Alkali said as he groaned slightly, trying not to show the surprise that he got when he found his limbs starting to move under his own power again as the venom wore off. "You were in such a hurry to try and stage the scene after you had broken in that you needed to use your own apparently favorite knife to kill him; I recognized it as the one that they had found as the murder weapon and that you had stolen from evidence after giving me the replacement tequila bottle, and then you had once more taken it back after replacing it with a kitchen knife before leaving with us."

"Mmm, I do enjoy this knife," Serathin said as he played with the tip of it with a claw. "I actually thought you had gotten suspicious with the glass inside the room when I broke in to take the python by surprise, looks like I cut myself for nothing."

"I noticed the glass, and guessed that you had deliberately smeared up your own file," Alkali said. "You were also the only one in the group that knew I was going to the safehouse when we met with Kage, and I'm guessing you popped Draggor's tire to attempt to stall us so you could take advantage of the knowledge we got from the Rat. The big mistake though was in the safehouse when you said that his throat was slit like the FBI agent while everyone else, including Uncle Kage, thought that he had been stabbed."

There was a moment of silence as the draconic sabrewolf looked at him in awe, then burst out laughing. "See, I knew that you were good!" Serathin said before his face fell serious and he pointed the gun at the ferret. "Shame it has to end like this. Nothing personal Alkali, I actually really like you, but you're going to take the blame for this one way or the other, if Kage finds out it was me all along than I'll be the one with a bullet in my head."

"No one is going to believe this!" Alkali shouted as Serathin moved over to his side and grabbed his arm, putting his finger in the space of the trigger on his gun.

"Oh… just like the police didn't think that those other three were suicides?" Serathin replied with a chuckle as he leaned in closer to the ferret's ear. "As you can see I'm very good at telling a story, and that's all the cops or the FBI or even your friends are going to care about. You can make anyone believe anything as long as you tell a good enough tale, something I'm sure that you're acutely aware of, and though you've been trying to rewrite the ending I'm afraid that I'm the one in control of the pen. After that the police will come and read how a distraught detective failed to prove his innocence and decided to end his own life instead of take the heat, it's a tale as old as time itself and a fitting epilogue to the end of your book."

Alkali felt the cool metal of his own gun being pressed to his head and even with the venom wearing off he couldn't gather the strength to push away the killer, his eyes squeezing shut as the draconic sabrewolf stood over him with a triumphant gleam in his eyes. A few seconds later the gunshot rang out like the bell of a cathedral, but when he didn't fall into the embrace of death the ferret opened his eyes to see a look of shock on the hybrid's face and a new hole in his clothes. As Serathin looked up with those green eyes he suddenly recoiled back as a second shot hit him where the first had landed, followed by a third and a forth that caused him to stagger back before he fell through the window with a loud crash. When Alkali looked at the source of the bullets he saw Trinity standing there with a smug grin on her face and the end of her revolver smoking slightly.

"How's that for an ending," Trinity said before she went over to Alkali. "You alright?"

"Cut it a little close there," Alkali replied as he attempted to sit up in his chair, clutching his chest as the wolfdog came up and helped straighten him up.

"I wanted to make sure we got the entirety of his confession taped," Trinity stated as she motioned back to where she had been hiding and recording everything as Alkali shivered slightly from the cold air that came swirling in from the busted window. "Also,

I honestly thought you might be dead. When I saw you take that knife to the chest I thought that I would have to be telling you that this plan to use yourself as bait was stupid while visiting your grave."

"Well when he didn't shoot at those gangsters I assumed that he didn't use guns," Alkali grunted as he reached in slowly with his arm and pulled out his watch, which had a thin slit-shaped hole that went clean through the timepiece. When he opened it he found the clock stuck right at midnight beneath the cracked, bloody glass before he shut it. "Glad I got this out of evidence, otherwise you would be avenging me instead of helping me right now… actually, you better go out there and cuff Serathin while you're at it so he doesn't escape Momma T."

Trinity gave Alkali a look of confusion before she went out and looked through the window, her face turning to shock before she reached out and dragged the struggling hybrid back inside and dropped him to the ground. As he let out a loud groan from the knee on his back she took out a pair of handcuffs and brought his hands together behind his body to restrain him. Once everything was in place she turned him over and opened the shirt that he wore to reveal a set of thin iron plates that were underneath with four areas severely dented. It had occurred to the detective that someone like Serathin might have done on purpose what happened to him by accident, seeing the scowl on the sabrewolf's lips as he was brought to his feet in front of the detective.

About an hour later the police had shown up and with Trinity's help they managed to make sure that not only did Alkali not get shot himself but also was cleared of the charges that were filed against him. Even though it was extremely cold out they stood on the street and watched as Serathin was led away in handcuffs, the hybrid looking over at Alkali with a slight smirk before he was brought to the police car. Before they could get him inside though alkali suddenly yelled, causing all the officers and the killer to look over at him in slight shock as he ran forward and put his fingers inside of the sabrewolf's muzzle to pry it open and look around. When he didn't see any strings tied to his teeth or tongue he nodded to the officers and told them he would be by later to provide his statement.

With that finished Alkali had a brief stop at a hospital for stitches before he got a ride with one of the officers to Club Anthrocon, going up to Uncle Kage's suite to tell him what happened. The cockroach listened intently while he poured from the bottle of tequila that had been left there previously, handing the clear liquor over to the ferret once he had finished. "I'll tell you that's the last time I hire outside help," Kage stated as he took a sip of his own wine. "It also explains why several associates of mine went to that speakeasy early, apparently Serathin had convinced them that you had already lapsed in your time and if they wanted to be in my good graces they would capture you dead or alive for me."

"He was a slippery one," Alkali replied after he had drained the majority of his glass and held it out for a refill since the hospital hadn't given him anything but a local anesthetic for his wound. "Admittedly using the FBI investigation as a smokescreen to do a real heist was clever, it's just they killed their patsy a little too early. The only reason he kept me alive after that was the hope that you'd hang all this around my neck and close the murder investigation with a neat little bow so you wouldn't take any revenge on him."

"Well I have a few people waiting for him to arrive at prison in order to make sure he knows the amount of debt he's in with me," Kage replied. "They'll put him to good use I'm sure to pay me back for the inconvenience that he's caused me."

Just as Alkali and Kage were about to get another refill on their drink the phone on the syndicate leader's desk began to ring. Instinctively the ferret went to check his watch only to remember that it had broken saving his life, but he knew that it was quite late for the cockroach to receive a phone call. Though it was hard to hear what was being said the detective could see that Kage's face was becoming more and more angry with each moment that the conversation passed by as he poured himself another drink and downed it quickly. Already he knew that whatever was being said to him on the other end was not good, an assumption that was strengthened when he slammed the receiver down so hard it almost broke the phone.

Though Alkali wanted to know what was happening he waited as Kage made a few more phone calls, then finally came back to where they were sitting. "It appears that our new mutual friend has decided he didn't enjoy the hospitality of the police," Kage explained as he sat back down. "I will have to make much different arrangements now."

"Wait… are you saying that Serathin managed to escape?" Alkali asked in shock.

"It appears that is the case," Kage replied angrily. "A call came into dispatch that caused the entire station to clear out, and by the time they realized it was fake and came back the holding cell they had put the sabrewolf in was open and he was gone. All they found inside was a piece of string."

Alkali sighed loudly as he realized that it was the same trick that he had pulled to get him out of the police station… with a slight variation. "You'll have to tell whatever officer handled that string that he's going to have to wash his hands," Alkali said as he stood up. "I'll leave you to the hunting, I'm going back to my office. I have a window to fix and I was going to meet someone there anyway."

Before Kage could say anything the ferret walked out of the office where a number of people had started to scramble in order to catch the escaped killer. It was unlikely that would happen, he thought to himself, and instead of wasting his energy to track a ghost he went back to his office to rest and recover from his ordeal. When he got there he saw that Trinity was just inside the main door waiting for him with a frown on her face. As part of the investigation she had just put in a requisition for special agents to handle the transfer of Serathin, but he had already slipped out of police custody before they could come down.

"FBI and ATF are working together to try and catch him before he leaves the city," Trinity stated as they walked up the stairs together. "He's only got a few minutes for a head start, hour at most, so maybe we'll get lucky."

"Doubt it," Alkali replied, sighing slightly as he could feel the cold air coming from his office even before he got to the door. "Someone like that knows how to escape nets, though I feel like we won't be seeing him anytime soon with the Syndicate and the alphabet agencies after him."

"What about you?" Trinity asked. "What are you going to do?"

"I'll just grab a few things and then go to Xander's," Alkali explained. "It's going to be a few days before I can get someone out here to fix the window and I don't feel like freezing to death after going through all this."

"You know what I mean," Trinity said as she pushed the ferret, who winced slightly and held the bandaged area on his chest. "Sorry, but I'm talking about what you're going to do if Serathin decides to take another swing at you. You managed to beat him this time but this hybrid is clearly a psychopath."

Alkali just shook his head as they got to the door of his office and the ferret fished out his keys to open the door. "There's no reason for him to go after me anymore," Alkali said. "The only reason he was doing it in the first place was to try and cover his tracks, the fact that everything is out in the open killing me will yield no benefit to him. He doesn't strike me as the type to try and get revenge, the way he talked this all seemed like a game to him, so I'll probably not see hair nor hide of him again."

"Are you sure about that?" Trinity commented as he opened the door to reveal his office with snow already drifting inside. What caused the wolfdog to say that was the full bottle of tequila that sat right in the middle of his desk. Alkali's eyes widened in surprise as he went over to it and picked it up, noticing it was the same kind that Serathin had originally stolen from him, and when he did he saw a piece of paper underneath. It was a note that had his name on it and after he handed the bottle to Trinity he opened it to read what's inside.

"Sorry that I had to ruin your ending but prison life just isn't for me," Alkali read out loud. "Hopefully you can accept this bottle as my way of saying that I hold no hard feelings for you, and also that you don't harbor any animosity towards me for trying to send you there myself… and for trying to kill you… twice. Don't worry, this one isn't poisoned. Signed, Serathin."

"Yep, psychopath," Trinity said as Alkali took the bottle back. "You're not honestly going to drink that, are you?"

"Of course not, it's prohibition after all," Alkali replied with a grin as he tossed it in the trash. Trinity just chuckled at that as he sat back down in his chair and looked around with his hands behind his head. Once more he was the lord of his domain, and though it didn't read it on the door until he got the window fixed it would still be the place where anyone could find the city's greatest detective.

THE END